Gott'im's Monster
1808

Gott'im's Monster 1808

S. Dorman

Published by S. Dorman, 2024.

Five books in THE GOD'S CYCLE
God's House:
Return to God's House
Within Without
In Winter

God's Wilderness:
Mystery Gottheim
Balder's Wilderness
Plus
Gott'im's Monster 1808
And
The Unabridged
Gott'im's Monster

Gott'im's Monster

1808

The Abridged Edition of
Gott'im's Monster
By S. Dorman

S. Dorman
    P.O. Box 172
    Greenwood, ME 04255
    USA
    Gott'im's Monster, 1808
    (An abridgement of *Gott'im's Monster*)
    By S. Dorman
    Copyright 2025 SusanDorman
    ISBN: 9798230937821

Dedication

To my family and friends

Many thanks for your kind encouragement.

"Eustace," remarked Mr. Pringle, after some deliberation, "I find it impossible to express such an opinion of this story as will be likely to gratify, in the smallest degree, your pride of authorship. Pray let me advise you never more to meddle with a classical myth. Your imagination is altogether Gothic, and will inevitably Gothicize everything that you touch. This giant, now! How can you have ventured to thrust his huge, disproportioned mass among the seemly outlines of Grecian fable?"

"I described the giant as he appeared to me," replied the student, rather piqued. "And, sir, if you would only bring your mind into such a relation with these fables as is necessary in order to remodel them, you would see at once that an old Greek had no more exclusive right to them than a modern Yankee has. They are the common property of the world, and of all time. The ancient poets remodelled them at pleasure, and held them plastic in their hands; and why should they not be plastic in my hands, as well?"

Mr. Pringle could not forbear a smile.

—Nathaniel Hawthorne, *A Wonder Book*

Contents

The Monster Appears

Dressed in buckskin and woolen stockings made by my mother, I was on Jasper Mountain many a day, camping, writing in my diary (especially when staying in the old hermit's camp), a failed young poet of eighteen winters in a harsh setting with privation. I comforted myself with the thought that at least I wasn't gone off on a Whaler—to get caught by the mad King and pressed into service in what was fast becoming the greatest naval empire ever known to man... unless Napoleon had anything to say of it. But then I recalled that over to home the harness was frayed, the ax wanted a new handle and the scythe needed sharpening. Instead I was writing in my journal, learning to live off what I could find in the woods, and making notes on medicinals. My path on one of these forays crossed that of Victor Besiegt. He was skeletal and wild, but half alive.

Victor Besiegt and I knew one another as children, but as mere acquaintances, me the younger by several years; for the town was large and wild and its village, only, central. Our schools were perforce far-flung. Jasper Mountain was, as it is now, great in the Town's midst but it was easy for a man to become lost, bewildered, in such a place as Gott'im was in those days. The town remained undeveloped except for what a settler could do with his own hands. One who suckled maple syrup along with his mother's milk (she was not the first to offer a breast dipped in syrup), was Victor Besiegt, who grew a studious child and became schoolmaster in the Town. Victor was ambitious not for worldly fame or fortune, perhaps, but desirous to study in secret and bring forth copious invention.

It was a curious thing: almost simultaneous with seeing Victor huddled in the roots of a great white pine, I looked up and saw a white robin singing against the dusty green of its boughs. I'd never seen such a thing before. I'm not sure I'd have noticed him if it weren't for that. Yes, it was an authentic robin for it had a robin's breast, though the rest shone white, and its song was unmistakable. Not the lovely liquid song you hear from its homelier sister the wood thrush, but a hopeful unmelodious chirping. Truly, these two creatures, one above the other, had me doubting my eyes and thinking I'd gone mad.

It took me a while to realize that this was the selfsame Victor Besiegt of Gottheim. I roused him, reassured him, made shavings, struck flint and had a little fire going right there among the rocks. Then I went off to get my pouch full of medicinals and the cooking pot. On my way back to him I slung some shot to fetch down three gray squirrels. By nightfall he was taking broth and thanking me by name.

"Then, are you—by chance, you are Mr. Besiegt? Victor Besiegt? Of the Twombly Road, east of Gott'im?" His hair was dark and wild, a beard of some days grown. "The schoolmaster...." It was spring, cold spring, and his suit of clothes was in tatters. The woolen blanket I gave him (fully aware that it was lousy), fire and broth, had stopped him shivering. He nodded. His brows were knit tight, and his eyes desolate. At that moment I was thinking that perhaps I might return into less wild environs and take up schoolmastering for I was turning wild-like and did not want to come to this.

I did not pester him with my curiosity. Instead, I began telling something of my thoughts and times in those wilds. Truly, I was grateful to have someone whose mind was cast a bit like mine to talk with... providing he wasn't woods queer. His true state would be revealed when his strength returned. I don't remember what I told him, having solely a glimpse in my mind of the firelight playing over his features as he lay resting, listening, sometimes with eyes closed, to my talk. When at last I discerned he slept, I ceased, and sat there scratching and meditating what had become of him.

Jasper Mountain is a powerful mysterious place. People often have scant conception of its mysteries. Studying the gaunt features of my sleeping acquaintance, I had no doubt of his respect for the great granite nether regions; for its grand sometimes glistening bald pate

which gathered weather to it as though a cloak for its mystery. It was
easier to die on Jasper Mountain than to live there. When I first came to
its wilder parts I had no thought that I should change, but as time went
on I found myself susceptible to its influence and could not remain the
same. Then I wanted above all to mature, find direction and achieve
some sort of merit. I hoped not to enhance my humanity, but to repay
it. Otherwise I would not *be* fully human. Woods queer is a definite
proposition for the hermit in the wild. I'm not sure it can be avoided,
but the setting and solitude promote introspection, I've no doubt, and
that is a sure way to self absorption. Vacancy, absence of mind,
withdrawal are all symptoms: How do you fit back into that
community of your fellows?

The Indians had a word for Jasper Mountain taking into account
its ferocious Jasperness, its purity and crystalline nature, and also its
weather-gathering properties. They did not of course worship it but
their word for it did acknowledge its separateness and greatness, and
a deep and abiding respect. It was a long, untidy, melodious word
and perhaps it was not a word at all but a phrase. Over the span of
a couple hundred years since my time many holes have been dug in
Jasper's sides trying to get at his multiplicity of crystal. Jasper has been
dynamited and bulldozed, even tunneled here and there, but back in
the beginning—the white people's beginning—there was nothing of
the sort done. The creatures inhabiting it then would think nothing
of such stuff. They would only be interested and involved in living,
and that would be enough: Now I live in the crystalline city, now I
see that that sort of living is enough to exercise of the imagination, of
spiritual and intellectual traits that a human might have. It is romantic
and realistic in one, without division to the human life.

Before falling asleep by the embers, I found myself drifting,
thinking speculatively about the white robin I'd seen earlier in the day,
surprised that I had forgotten it. *How could you forget a thing like a
white robin?*

About the time of this story, some thirty years after the Twitchells laid out the town, there was a glass case in Dr. Kimball's house: Dr. Kimball's was the second house in the town to have real glazed windows, too. This was a fancy walnut glazed cabinet with shelves full of curiosities; and even monsters, you might say, were there displayed. I'm fairly certain he had written papers on each one of these abnormalities of nature, not all by any means found in the area of Jasper Mountain. Many of these creatures were from away somewhere in different locales of the known New World geography. Five-footed kittens, tiny two-headed piglets, birds born without wings, pickled Siamese twin embryos of some suggestive kind or other. (It always made me feel... queer to see them.) I found myself wondering if perhaps the Doctor might like to add the white robin to his collection. But would it be just a curiosity, might not it also serve the natural science? Could not we learn more about our world through a study of it?

I knew in another moment I'd be fired by the idea and try to do something about it: but as I drifted off I heard again its unlovely pretense of a song in my head, saw it living there on the branch. I had to snort at myself: a stuffed white robin in the case and dissected on paper or a live robin flying around and procreating— white or not? Was there really some choice in this? (I did not hardly notice my thought that the former plan was sure to make a good impression on a very influential man in the community. One whose further acquaintance was certain to have a good influence on a literary profession, for someone who wanted to see his poetry in the broadsheets... as opposed to farming the field or birching the backsides of recalcitrant school children.)

In dim morning robin song woke me from somewhere above. It was no white robin, for I would have seen its illumination; instead I but heard its squealing song. I lay staring into the branches as day lightened, thinking of my determination to do well. I was confident now that I wanted to work with my mind, but from the impetus of my heart, freely. Not dryly, not analytically. But not as a poet, either. That had to be given over.

I propped myself on an elbow upon my heap of pine twigs and scrutinized Victor. His breathing indicated a healthy sleep. A deep sleep, but that notwithstanding I began to think that I would be caring for him some days. He too lay on pine needles to keep him against the damp. He wore my coat and was wrapped to the chin in one of my wool blankets made by Aunt Anna. I had the other, which I now threw aside. I squatted to the fire and began remaking it with what lay at hand before going to fetch more sticks.

It was two days before he could give an account of himself. In that time I had built a rude shelter right there, a ridge pole wedged in the crotch of a sapling and laid with poles lashed together, these in their turn overlaid with fir boughs, and latched tight with some buckskin strips. During the times of strengthening I spoke often, even sang to him, thinking that to do so might help restore his soul, even as his body gained. I remember singing "American Taxation," one of the ballads of the American Revolution:

While I relate my story, Americans give ear,
Of Britain's fading glory you presently shall hear;
I'll give a true relation, attend to what I say,
Concerning the taxation of North America.

I could not remember above six stanzas but it were well for both him and me: It was a monster of composition, upwards of 30 stanzas. I sang also "Springfield Mountain,"

Down to the mountain for to mow
He mowed, he mowed all around the field
With a poisonous serpent at his heel,

the story of Timothy Myrick of Massachusetts who was bitten by a snake and died while mowing the hay of his hillside farm. I even sang some sweet and sentimental parlor songs just then coming into vogue. But perhaps all this noise just vexed him. At first he seemed rested, then encouraged, but later I deem it all wearied him. Then I saw he was preoccupied, then troubled. Finally I forbore no longer and asked him outright what was wrong.

Having eaten nearly a whole roast of spring partridge, he was sitting up under the tree, lying against the hoary bark of the same white pine, there in the crooks where I'd found him. He shifted his gaze from his inwardness toward me, swiftly. I could see him working whether or no to unburthen himself. Idea and sensation passed through his countenance: of horror, of the pensive, of grief or regret, all this swiftly as he considered.

Then, without spirit, he said, "I scarcely know where to begin, Abner." He stopped and looked about, his dark eyes helpless in his beard-darkened face. At last he said, "This place is very harsh, this Jasper Mountain. It has tried to kill me, and I am sorry it has failed." He looked at me then, almost accusingly. But his glance softened and he looked away. In some exhaustion, softly he said, "But I thank you, pioneer youth. Abner."

On one impetus I wanted both to relieve him and yet lead him to continue. So I said, "May be you could start with your clothes. Tatters they are, but discernibly tailormade. You've been in the city, Cambridge was it? I know you are no longer teaching school in the Town." I could not keep the eagerness from my voice as I asked about these things. He had come out of himself enough to notice.

"Yes, I have been in the college. Would you aspire to such a place, such learning? If so," he looked at me with penetration, "take care, Abner. Even a little learning can make one mad. I'm not sure but what 'a little' may be, in some instances, more dangerous than much learning.... I have uncovered much that was secret—yet now I feel I've learned little if anything of importance... but solely how to *deepen* the curse natural to us. Take care, pioneer youth."

I lowered my eyes, despairing: There is no pain *like* wounded pride, such as I had come out into Jasper Mountain wilderness to assuage.

Now I was more desirous than ever to press him for what had happened, still I held back. "What did you study, how did you live?"

He hesitated. His gaze dropped to the crooks in which he sat. He picked up a scale of thick bark and began pulling it to pieces. "I studied galvanism, electricity. So as not to burden my father, and to earn my bread, I worked for the undertaker. I lived and studied in the top of his establishment. And my work both here and in the college laboratories put me in touch with all things needful for my true... work." He seemed to suppress a shudder. Victor Besiegt sat quietly, watching me. Assessing me, I thought.

I was keen to ask him about these strange subjects but his scarcely suppressed agitation checked me. "Were you all alone? Had you no friends?" I wondered if it were possible to go woods queer in the midst of many people —as if, among so many, one could be subject as though in a type of wilderness. I had read of Boston and New York, and been to fledgling Bangor for a day. My experience led only to surmise what it might mean to live *en masse*. I imagined what it must be like for a moose to wander into the city.

"I—have a dear friend, Henry Clairson, a fellow student. At first we saw one another regularly and supped almost nightly at a tavern in the square. I did not see many of my fellow natural science students, but was attracted to those in the Classics, liberal studies, and the fine arts. There was a wonderful school for the latter nearby. Clairson was a grammarian and had studied the poets copiously. I had another friend in the medical school, Percy Blake, and often we had fascinating conversations on human anatomy. He could draw well. His diagrams were astonishing.... You are a poet, Abner? There is little harm in it."

To fail at it may be, I thought but said nothing of that. "What great learning you have encountered! Anatomy, galvanism, electricity." I was not repulsed by his handling of the dead. In those days in Gottheim we thought nothing of undertaking, having not yet acquired a man or woman of that profession for preparing the dead in the village. This was something we did for one another in our homes, washing, dressing, and laying out the dead, waking, and attending the graveside service. My Aunt Anna kept an abundant supply, fresh in season, dried without, of rosemary and tansy to ward off unwholesome airs should the burying be untimely. I had borne the coffin for three or four elders and many babes in my time and helped to lower them into the rocky earth.

Bluntly he said, "That is a leading statement, Abner."

I stared at him, staying my course.

He stared at me.

Here might be a good place to remind the reader of certain characteristics of Yankee temperament derived from the Anglo-Saxons, with a nice overlay of Puritanism. Which of the two of us were to feel the more guilt, the more shame in his nature? Now that I am able to frequent the heavenly city, and to write of such things, I know almost the whole of the story of Gott'im's monster. I know what part Victor Besiegt played in its creation. But when I found him in the wilderness he was at first in no shape, and then soon *unwilling* to reveal much of anything of what he had done. For another thing, you must know the nature of insular Gott'im and how its primary form of entertainment, in the most casual way, and almost continually, is gossip. Its formal aspect springs out of the soil of character and pride whenever and wherever at least two people meet: oral, superficially fraternal, judgmental, reckless and frequently gleeful. The truth is, most of us don't even realize we are doing it. How casually and on what scant grounds we destroy the reputations of others. How could Victor, especially not knowing me well, share such a monstrous secret with me and trust that it would go no further; no matter how great the pressure on him to disclose, to unburthen? Here you have for my part no knowledge of what he had done. But we both knew what I had just done. I lowered my gaze and did not discern until we met at the judgment that he also turned away.

Notice the tension between the desire for friendship, intellectual and emotional kinship, and fear of the baser qualities that are part of the natural man. A monster of another sort had really come between us despite our need and my nursing of him, and we were helpless in those moments to work together to fend it off. We began to speak of other things.

"Have you seen a white robin?" I asked at last. The dim afternoon had waned and I had to make up the fire. I blew on the embers and glanced up through the small kindling flames. "There was one chirping in the branches up above you when I found you. I'm not sure, but it may be that I would not have noticed you there had I not seen it first."

"No. No, I haven't seen it." His gaze was again listless and absent. Then, perhaps to make up for his former hardness, he would confess at least something: "I haven't seen much of anything... since being so occupied... as you've apprehended. Abner, I'm chasing a monster."

I looked at him. Ridiculously, I think. I must have gawped. *Woods queer.*

He shut his eyes. "I can say no more."

I left him there and went off to check my snares in the half light, turning his conversation over in my mind. I now believed he was touched in some manner I could not clearly discern. Victor was lucid, normal in every way except for his nerves—and that last telling sentence about chasing monsters. He had talked of being unable to regain the semblance of life, despite his studies and accomplishments in Cambridge. Though I had come here into these wilds something of an uneasy man, he seemed to think I was in similar danger of ending like him. His speech was full of dire but general warnings. Could Education be such a bad thing, I wondered. When he himself had grasped it with both hands and with but a natural hunger? Surely that cannot account for his trouble?

I stooped to one of my snares and found it had gone off but was empty. Whatever he had done he should confess, no matter the price to himself, for only then (I thought) would he regain his balance. I mused, Can his friends have played a role in it? He must keep his secret. No matter how I have helped him, no matter my own desire for a friend (which he must plainly see), he will keep his secret. For whatever it is he has done he has done in secret. So how can our relation be other than coldly courteous?... on the other hand, in his extremity... he may yet unburthen himself.

It was a chill spring evening, which in this rocky north and wild means scant pickings in the bottom of the barrel even in our industrious communities, where salt meat in that barrel is almost gone by this time if not thoroughly consumed. Even were I over to home I would be setting snares for squirrel, for rabbits, even for fish. Snaring small game is one of the best ways to get meat from the wild for it takes not much energy, requires no firearm nor shot of any kind, and can prove abundant. So I set snares plentifully, routinely, and was seldom disappointed of a meal.

In the woods you will frequently find an old stump or small clearing beneath a tree as though showered with acorn husks. Look up into the tree above and if you see a big nest in a crook you know you are in the right neighborhood. Still, for all the ease of ensnaring these critters (to me far tastier than rabbit which is tough and tasteless), it is sad to see one hanging there on a rigged twig he took for a convenient limb.

Half light, as the saying goes, is better than no light in the woods but it's the kind of light could play tricks on your eyes, tricks in your mind, tricks along the nerves of even a seasoned trapper. I was working my way along the route I had set up since finding Besiegt and was coming up empty-handed. Not the usual thing. And the little nooses smelled bloodied and were torn. Then I came across the carcass of a squirrel that had been but partly eaten out and left in a ruinous little heap. I picked it up, fascinated, but it was too dark now to learn anything of it.

I looked through the forest of bare branches up toward the great light that was beginning low on this side of the mountain, the great white light of the moon. There, passing over bald rock I saw with complete fascination a sight I have never forgotten. The instant I saw it, I knew it was Besiegt's monster.

I wrote about it later in my diary, and it was handed down as legend in the oral annals of Gottheim. But naturally things don't carry well that way. For instance, here's a bit of conversation overheard recently as I was ghosting through Gott'im:

"He wrote that the monster was about the size of a horse with a long narrow face like one. Real heavy and clumsy."

"The horse face'n wearing long blond hair, said another. *"Usual description of Gott'im's monstah, but not always. Sometimes he's black as coal with a high forehead and taller than a moose maple at full height, on account of his flesh being made of corpses and his legs of two or three men stacked one on tother. Other times he's like you or me and caunt tell'im from anabody."*

Such a pieced-out plaguéd bit of nonsense that is. But they have fun with it. That keeps the legend alive. —In turn, helping Gott'imites figure out what goes on in their own time, wouldn't you say?

Trembling, tripping over deadfall, I had made my way back to camp. "Look at this," I said, laying my gruesome find near the fire. I watched him. "Not fit to eat."

Besiegt was awake when I returned. He went up on his knees and stared down at the little torn carcasses in fascination. He looked up at me then. "Yes."

He sat back again against the tree. "I told you."

"So a monster did this." It was my turn to suppress a shudder. I began to pace about the fire. "Victor, I've seen it...." I whispered: "I can scarcely believe I've seen it." I did shudder, I trembled. "Where—where did it come from? How can it be? Oh," I began to babble, "I have heard stories in my life, but never—oh, how did it get in these woods of

Gott'im. What is it doing on Jasper Mountain?" I think I raved a bit, before standing silent before him. Perhaps the look I cast on him was a hurt look, an accusing look.

I did not understand until much later the import of many of our conversations to follow in the days to come. Some, even, of the things *I* said in those times remained mysterious to me until I grew old and thought deeply.

"Will it get into the village, will it hurt anyone there?" The firelight glowed over the opening of the shelter, and remains of his meal, near where I'd set the torn squirrels. I gestured toward their shreds, my gaze still on him.

He had been looking away, silent as I roved to and fro. Now he looked at me. His voice was quiet. "He has been there. He has—not hurt anyone—there."

I gaped at him, wondering if he'd been about to say *yet*, instead of *there*. But absently my hand slipped into my shirt to scratch.

"Sit down, Abner."

I sat down, the small flames between us. Each had his firelit gaze upon the other. Slowly he began: "Being is too much for us, Abner. Too much responsibility in being alive.... not that being human excuses us from responsibility, but it is good, at least, that we understand this truth."

I almost shouted. "Stop with your learnéd abstractions! Tell me what you've done!"

Silence.

Then, "I made him." It was said very low. His mouth, surrounded by dark whiskers, closed in a firm straight line.

At the time I scarcely noticed his demeanor or mine, however. I could only think of the strangely disjointed monster with hair like a cape; of the village, my family, this happenstance. Happenstance? What was he saying? I continued gawping. "You—?"

"I made him."

My thoughts charged this way and that. I said, "... I heard once of a young ignorant boy who'd grown up in a household of vile people and knew nothing of the written word, of stories. He happened to stray into a hall once and heard a man reading from a book. All ragged and dirty, he went up to that speaker after the reading and demanded to know how he had put those pictures in his head. And not pictures only, but a whole experience. Oh, I hate saying this, Victor, but maybe you've done something of the sort to me. Did I really see that thing?"

"Yes. Abner, I will tell you—but not in instructive detail—how I made him. My words will make no manual. I'll never tell anyone how it was done."

As he began to speak, I recalled with one part of my mind the piece of amber I'd seen among Dr. Kimball's collection of oddities, and my excitement over experiencing its electric properties. You could rub it to produce sparks, you could make your hair stand on end. Victor was speaking, his voice quickening as he continued, his own words galvanizing Victor's thought and his fire-struck countenance and form.

Victor Begins

You will find this hard to believe, Abner, but we are a soup. Human beings are made largely of water with a small but immeasurably complex mixture of other ingredients in which electricity plays a major role in keeping us together, alive—and even separate from one another. I knew that if I studied it, worked diligently, and could lay hands on the right materials... such as the vivisectionist, anatomists, and undertakers come in the way of... I could... *make*... a living being, a new creation. Yes, make. You must have read of Luigi Galvani and his experiments with frogs on a metal lattice during thunderstorms. Volta came along and was able to drive current, the electromotive force, through his voltaic pile. He proved the reciprocity between electricity and chemical reaction.

I scarcely know what— possessed me, but I *was* possessed of a most exhilarating mania of effort to bring forth that horrible creature. Now I can only shake my head in wonder over it. Wonder over *myself, the ultimate mystery*. But I have learned so much since then— not what I am capable of, but what I am *incapable* of. I think that was it: I wanted to prove myself capable beyond my abilities, and have since had to conclude that it was arrogance. Now I know my arrogance, but not its cure.

On the day of the monster's— birth (I use that word!— it was *his* word!) —I had been working my strength out for days. He lay on the metallic lattice I had prepared for him, his stitched together flesh and sinew, not yet two days gone in death and since held in ice, still well preserved. I should've known in just looking down on his fascinating form.... Abner, how much the creation is made of beauty! It is the whole covering of beauty.... But the monster was ugliness *and* beauty personified. I felt a slight impress to stop.... —If only I had heeded. Just that one moment —hesitate!

I had created in my makeshift laboratory a massive voltaic pile of alternating layers of zinc and pasteboard soaked in salt water and silver, but before the current was well used I saw that there wasn't enough force to jolt him to life. I thought if I added more layers to the pile.... I had been working feverishly and was so disappointed, too overwrought to notice the atmosphere without the house. Oddly, it seems to have noticed me and what I was doing. Perhaps all that effort and devoted workmanship, the exultation of what I might do with hands and mind spoke to the elements, the ether, I don't know. Sounds superstitious, does it not? *I have been turned on my head.* The room was shut there at the top of the house but that did not stop the lightning. Ball lightning, Abner! The windows and doors were blown open. I was knocked to my knees, deafened. Men of science have disputed its existence but it is real, Abner, real. It appeared through the air of the room with astonishing colored brightness, hissing, softly snapping, and swiftly galvanized the whole form of that awful makeshift being. You ask how can it *be*. I too ask that, Abner.

You may (or at least your mother will) remember my father, Almon, as a man who was already well into middle age when he came into Farmingham Royal, as it was then known. A professional man in Boston, he married late in life and had me in consequence. He retired here in order to work on his metaphysical treatises. Here I was born, and here grew to an age with my adoptive sister, Regina, the daughter of friends of my mother. You will remember her: delicate, refined, quietly beautiful. Closer your age. When I left here our betrothal was more felt that acknowledged. ...And you may remember my brother, Greenleaf. He is a good lad, but thinks too highly of me. I have betrayed his worship. My mother was poor but educated, the daughter of my father's colleague in the college. She was sensitive to deprivation and with a good will desired to spare Regina growing up in want. My mother— my mother died and my father was left alone to raise us. We were privileged enough, as you know, to have household help. I did not go to school for my father taught us, and his library was mine to plunder. Larger even than that of Dr. Kimball, I suspect you've heard of this library: Nothing escapes the notice of Gott'imites.

I reveled in the works of Cornelius Agrippa, Paracelsus, and Albertus Magnus. Alchemy, the art of the Egyptians, intrigued me, and the study of electricity was the study of marvels. What marvels for the scientists in the invisible! Franklin, Priestley, Coulomb. While Regina was content to observe and read, I had to put hand and thought into everything of interest to me. She did not take part in my experiments, but would often come and sit near in the workshop, my makeshift laboratory, perched on a stool, watching. Greenleaf wanted to see what I was about, but he was too young for this then.

Father doted on me, and encouraged my studies, but he could be demanding, too, if he thought it were in my best interest. He might have pushed me further into obsession, but instead chose to seek nourishment for that part of me he would've thought belonged to my mother, that of compassionate service to others. So I served for a time as the schoolmaster in West Gottheim, only to please him. And perhaps to keep peace in the household. But after awhile I insisted on going to the college. And, having satisfied his conscience, he let me go, deeply interested to nourish the flourishing of my faculties.

At Harvard College I met Henry Clairson, a poet, mythologist, and student of literature. We became close, chiefly because of his great sympathy and sensitivity, but I was never able to duplicate or reciprocate the quality of his caring; a true friend. I'm sure that I knew more about him and cared less; he knew less of me and cared more. He knew of course that I was experimenting but, for all his speculative and romantic imagination, would never have dreamed what I was about.

I'm telling *you*, Abner, for the most practical of reasons. I need your help. My secrecy, above anything else except for the accursed invention, has brought more destruction than is bearable.... And I feel now a sort of relief, such as Catholics must feel when they come out of the confessional. —But I am not done confessing.

You think, What has it all to do with the monster. You think, Get Victor back on his feet and let's go after and kill that thing. It's not so easy, Abner. Life, *being* is too complex for that. You've no idea. But yes, enough damage has been done to warrant it, if only you will listen to me tell this awful thing complete: Then you will be motivated to kill another—I don't say human, but I am sure when it comes to the point, you will need more... more justification for your conscience. Yet I'm half-tempted to let you go ahead after him without the story. For when you have the full story, you will see just how human he is. Yes, if you went now, you may be so steeped in horror of his looks and manner that firing a shot into him may yet be perceived a mercy.... And perhaps either way it would be. It will be, I'm convinced, a mercy to all that he be destroyed. (And he not least.)

Yes. Yes. I see it now. It is you who must aim, fire shot. How much better if you had one of the new breech-loading fire arms. I doubt these can have come into the hardscrabble woods as yet?... Well then you will have to go home to fetch your flintlock musket, since you have one. For you *will* need it. None of your primitive weaponry for him. Yes, his strength and agility, you will find, are daunting, phenomenal.

I've been thinking carefully of Regina. She must be saved at all costs.... Yes, well naturally you will want to spare the whole village his presence, but understand there is a particular reason why she— I will tell you later. I must compress the background now and be done with it. It is necessary, but full disclosure will come. Right now let me just say I owe her a great debt for taking charge of the household at a young age and overseeing the comfort of the family. It was my mother's wish that we marry, as well as my own, and this will happen yet if we can rid the world of the monster.

...In the college I learned of my "stupidity" in being entranced with alchemy. There I was told that it was a false science, but the ridicule did not stop me: I knew from an early age that I wanted to make a living being, that it would be a service to humanity and perhaps promote human longevity. Before I tell you about my strange encounter with the living offshoot of my imagination, let me say that I did have one instructor who did not disparage my early studies of alchemy. Professor Waldmann did not chastise me as had others, deploring my lack of science, but pointed out what was of value and encouraged me to apply rigor to other branches, even mathematics, and steep myself in true science. I did so, and before I began my great work gained a reputation for thoroughness and understanding with my professors, and even among my fellow students.

My single-minded study then became so involving, so rewarding of my passion: a complete reciprocity between passion and studies, bringing not only my *object* to life, but myself as well: but in a way that proved lopsided. I would have to say it was even as my father had feared. The side of me that had belonged to my mother was transmuted, and I was able to believe that her devotion to service was now in me as the type of service toward the good of my fellows. I reveled in giving my all to this great service. An exploration of the mystery of human life. A new *being*. The creation of a new race of men. And an opportunity for the perfection of it. Have I found the incipient means of renewal of life whereby we may escape corruption of the body?—

If so, the price is too great. Unlike the most recent Dr. Faustus I will not have my redemption for I do not believe in divine intercession. If it exists it's too weak. The divine has abdicated to its inferior, allowing might to preside over being.

Had I been applying the same rigor to my own life as to my project, I would have seen the evidence of my wrongheadedness: I lost touch completely for months at a time with the people I love, the friends who liked and respected me, the enjoyment of nature, and human comforts to be found in small pleasures and congenial society. Unanswered correspondence overflowed the table beside the door. I stopped writing to my father and brother; even my intended was neglected, she who might have been able to share in my discoveries—had I not been enthralled with the accursed invention. There was more evidence: I would never have told Regina my plan. My very secrecy was proof that part of me understood the horror I was cooking up for myself. And for the community of my fellows. How much better it is for you, Abner, whose whole world and life is Gottheim. Seek not to change it.

Abner, if I neglected to coordinate the various elements of my well-being... I must even ask myself if I am *incapable* of such responsibility—Oh the tediousness of such a job when what one wants is the thrill of one's own pursuit! Abner, it is too much! And here I have been making a being *not myself.* I who cannot understand nor master my own being. Can we truly separate out the good from the evil of our studies, our techniques and inventions? Can we say, Ah yes, here is an evil use, there a good, I will be sure to follow the good and reject the evil use? If there is a divine voice anywhere, would not that voice speak to us, guide us? If I heard it, Abner, it was too slight, feeble, ineffectual. How can such a thing stop the brave reckless power of passion? ...If only I had listened.... But I perhaps blame it on a weak conscience, when I should say instead that I disregarded what was perhaps a pure faculty. Had it been an iron hand grabbing hold of my arm to stop the experiment... perhaps.... But then... would I have been eaten up in anger at being thus thwarted?

Right about then Abner Bartlett, the one who had to listen to this, was thwarted. I wanted to slap the silliness out of him, and said so. "I'm tempted to relieve you of being, Victor. If you don't tell me about this monster I'm going to force that torn squirrel down your gibbering gullet! Not only has too much learning made you mad but it's making me mad now, too."

I did not say that at any other time I would have been listening intently to his speaking, as to a poetic discourse. That would have been too much encouragement. I was very uneasy.

"I'm going for more wood for that fire. —Is it waiting for you? Will it be aimlessly wandering the mountain? Does it have a mind to plot? *What* would it plot? When I come back you will have gathered your wits together and come up with a plan for us, one that includes a description of what I will be facing out there."

I stalked off into the night-shadowed woodland, careful of my footing in the trackless brush. I did not want inadvertently to step on a skunk, porcupine, or other apparently but not actually harmless slow creature. That would have thrown the whole process back; and destroyed my dignity. Of which I was rather proud at that moment—having spoken up to so eminent a personage as that. Called him by his Christian name, too!

The moon was now high, turning the woodland into a solemn dreamscape such as my quill would have reveled in at another time. The barely leafing hardwoods lay their shadows downslope at angles off their dark trunks. Below me the moonlit side of them was white, silver, and gray, striped with shades. The slope above me steepened and I saw the white disc through many branches pouring its light down through the rich geometry of still great shadow-beings, the trees. I began gathering an armload of small dry deadfall not overfar from camp. The still night was touched with a faint bad smell, as though from a great distance. Quickly it strengthened with sinister potency: the smell of skunk unleashing its full weaponry. It drifted down slope on the falling night air. I paused to wonder, *What is its target?*

"Keep steady, Abner. It's only a skunk defending itself against some woodland canine. Maybe it's tangling with a bear: double the poisonous odor to me, in that wise. A bear out of hibernation— *phew.*" All this was said in a nervous murmur meant for calming. I climbed up through the trees with half an armload. I had cut short Victor Besiegt's talk partly from a nervous reaction to our inaction, and gathering the wood had been soothing to me. But now, again stooping to my task, I felt the same thrill I'd had in my brief glimpse of the monster as it strode the mountainside. I gathered every stick near to hand and stood.

I heard something. I turned. In the patterned white light and shadow stood the monster, his great form barred with these striping contrasts where he stood against a tall fir. His patterned, scarred face was illumined by a moonbeam, but what shocked me was the swift recognition of —.

At first I thought he was bearded. Any normal man would have been blinded by the toxins in the white, almost pure white, skunk he gripped in his teeth. This was a man of astonishing proportions with gleaming long hair, at once tall and broad-shouldered but with arms and legs fantastically jointed. He was actually handsome—no, beautiful—in a strange way. But all these impressions came later.

At that moment the life went out of the creature in his mouth. Calmly the monster eyed me with a look of jet as he clenched down, tore at it, and pulled the skunk away with his great hand. I did not wait to watch him chew, but dropped the wood and fled.

I scrambled without heed through the puckerbrush. At the moment I had no thought but to get away beneath the trees, and after a time of such work through the tangles, my mind came back to me. Still thrashing about, I tried to think what to do. I felt I'd been gone from camp for hours and, but for the clawing of the puckerbrush, my throes, the disembodied whining of someone's mouth (my own), I'd have called it a dream.

I paused, listening, then moved along quickly but now with quiet detachment. Nothing had come after to hinder me. Nothing was chasing me. I merely needed to find Victor Besiegt and tell him what I'd seen. If I could do that... maybe I would stop seeing it.

I saw clearly the value of having another, a believer, who shared the nightmare. One who might help me destroy it. No, hearer, don't think I did not consider running away. You will know better than to think I wanted no escape: that I did not long to get away: from Jasper Mountain, from Gott'im altogether and just vanish, just make my way to outlandish New Orleans or some other worldly and bewildering place. All this came into my mind, a sane mind, that. That was the normal thing. But it was the thing that could not, must not, be.

He had to be destroyed.

He? Now it occurred to me (still with my eyes searching to and fro) that when I saw Dr. Besiegt's monster I recognized the man in him, enough to use the personal pronoun. Up until then that was not the case. Maybe that was why I was so scared.—No, I was horrified. I had never known horror before.

I saw fire light distantly, and found camp again in its little dell with moonlight. I saw that Victor had been up and able to keep the fire going on his own. He looked up startled at my wild approach.

"I know now—he *is* for you."

"Yes—"

I was wild, moving about, gesticulating. I kicked a bit at the fire and said (but I could not keep the admiration out of my voice), "He's invincible!— He had this skunk." I must've gibbered. One part of my mind admired Victor's handiwork excessively. "On seeing him, that skunk in his mouth, a white one.... the stench and.... I was struck... ran off."

Silence.

Victor, sitting among the roots, leaned back against the trunk and closed his eyes. Shadow washed over his face.

"Why doesn't he just come here and get you, then?"

I sensed his deep reluctance. At last he said, "As you said. He's waiting." Besiegt stopped.

"He won't go to Gott'im? Not till he's done with you? He does plot."

"Yes. He can do everything. ...How those words would have thrilled me had I heard them two years ago at this time." His gaze slid to the small fire and he put his knuckles to his mouth, gnawing on them absently, distraught. He took his hand away and looked up at me. "You will help me? Abner. I've taught him nothing. He has learned all through others. You said his beauty, but as he lay there pinned with wires after the lightning—*living*, his breath convulsing, opening his jet eyes—I was struck with horror. Abner, I ran off."

He looked at me, and for the first time I sensed shame. But I could hardly believe what he had said. "You... made him. —And ran off? That was the *first* thing you did?" I laughed. I could not have kept that laughter back. But it was bitter. It was hard to keep scorn out. Not in scorn, but in bitterness I said, "Well, *Doctor* Besiegt, since your marvelous creation is waiting on its master-smart maker, maybe you can tell me how he learned —what, and why he is waiting. And what we will do about it. From your cryptic hints, it sounds like he's been to Gott'im with some intention or other."

He sighed. "It's a long story. A long night for you, Abner."

"I assure you, I will not be sleeping any time soon. Proceed."

Family and Friends

The atmosphere of the room had changed, the ozone smell having cleared out, the storm passed away. There was a great calm. He awoke. There was no struggle as with a newborn babe. Life was in him, he moved, he open his eyes, and I ran off. Horrified. I waited for nothing, just ran blindly down the stairs, staggered into the street. Already the weekday crowds were thronging it after the storm. They stepped aside as wildly I splashed through puddles. I was probably much as you were in the wood there after seeing him. I was wild as you were.

Somehow, after perhaps hours (I remember hurrying along the Charles River and over the bridge but don't remember coming back), I found myself dragging slowly up the stairs to Clairson's rooms. I wondered: What am I going to do with myself? I did not think, What am I going to do with this monster. The thought never entered my mind. Such relief I felt in Henry's instant sympathy. It was balm to me, as though the rest of God were opened, and I had but to enter in. He sought to relieve my evident distress and plied me with every kindness. What a man he is.

[As your guide through the story of Gott'im's monster, I Abner will tell you that I met Henry Clairson in that heavenly city I told you of, and we knew one another's minds instantly on the subject of Victor. Not only the glimmering streets, through which we see earth, but our very selves are transparent to one another for the flame of light in our eyes by which we see everything. Nothing of this sort is hidden. Redemption is a thing so far beyond the English language as to be indescribable to you in your night, and darkly fallen condition; but I will say that unlike some, or even most of the redeemed, Henry Clairson, was not that much changed from the description given above and below by his friend.]

If you have had any trial at all in your life, Abner, you will know the virtue of even a kindly *silent* presence with you in it, whether you give voice to the trouble or not. That person, just being near, will work a wonder on your psyche. You must know this, if, as I remember, you grew up in a kindly family. Though Henry himself was distressed to see me so, and would have inquired deeply and intently in order to be of better use, his native courtesy, nay, his kindness, forbade him. And I could not bring myself to speak of my experience, nor confess what I had done. So great was my befuddlement, so irritated my nerves, that he suggested I stay with him the night, and promised to see me settle quietly in my rooms the next day. Of course I wanted none of the latter, but forbore speaking of it. I acquiesced with deep gratitude to his offer of hospitality.

Abner, in all this terrible trial, I've confided in not one soul till now. I tell you what a relief it is, at last, to have someone to share it with. I see now what Vico the great historian was after with his insistence on understanding or empathy. It was part of his methodology. Experimentation is the thing, yes, but how much use is it when we are solely imitating nature? But we are humans, and what humans *make*, *that* is what we need understanding of. He believed in the cyclical history, not the delusion of what we will call progress, the moving from what is lesser or inferior to what is greater or better. We need understanding because we cannot even know ourselves, nor (as Descartes thought), truly, know of our existence.

But we should be able to know, or to experiment upon, or to study deeply, what we ourselves have made. And this is where I failed, and do fail to this day. It was not that all this was beyond Henry, but that Henry was beyond this. He did not so much know, according to philosophy, *about* the qualities that make life worth living but he *embodied* them, expressed them. And he knew of them as poetry. Such as the Greeks and Romans knew of these things: truly as poets and not as philosophers. He would never have been the "father" of such a thing, not possibly. But had he inherited this monster, as a foster father, he would have known what to do with him. Oh yes, like God, man is the maker, but just about any old man can make. Perhaps fewer men can be true fathers.

The next day we approached the undertaker's house in which I dwelt in the top rooms, and you may imagine my loathsome shrinking—and speculation, reluctance to speak—all fogged with torpor, which I could not possibly express to my friend. He sensed the fever in my nerves and spoke lightly, gently, but with his own trepidation for my condition. Can you imagine? With every step rising into the upper reaches of the house, I shuddered, knowing not what to say, nor even how to prepare my friend. My shattered state but prepared him for encroaching illness, not the sight of *that* awaiting us.

Together we entered, he urged me to sit and rest, offering to fetch the woman to bring refreshment; but trembling I declined, saying I was not hungry. We sat there in my little furnished parlor, and I refused speaking, silence settling on us. Everything in me strained, listening toward the upper chamber. No sound came to us, and at last, pleading exhaustion, again I expressed my thanks, promised to rest and receive him again on the morrow; as softly he withdrew, still with that look of deep gentle concern.

When he was gone I sank back, listening again. Silence filled the upper chambers but for the ticking of the clock on the secretary. The hope grew in me that my creation had been flawed and unable to sustain the life that had been ignited in him. I sat there for perhaps an hour, my nerves in a terrible state, and then slowly I rose and opened the door, mounted the narrow stair. I entered the laboratory.

He was gone.

I stood trembling, looking at the strung iron lattice which helped bring him to life. I willed it for a dream, but saw the evidence of his life everywhere, the tables and instruments in complete shambles, so much debris on the floor; the voltaic pile no longer apparent except in pieces scattered among the— there was everything made by man for his scientific, industrial and technical purposes; pieces, once refined out of the raw elements of the earth we have inherited and are now using in whatever way we will. All wreckage, everything destroyed. I went to the broken windows and looked out. The shutter hung open, gaping, and I wondered.

"Abner, we can know about something or know something. These are two different types of knowledge, but for some of us it is long before we learn this distinction. The first has to do with reason, logic, and rote understanding. The second is experience. Until that day, before I looked out that window for traces of the monster, I had been busily, feverishly, trying to bring about being; someone else's being. Now, for the first time, I am becoming aware of my own, and it is painful. I can't tell you how painful. But this was only the beginning of my laborious knowing *experience* of my difficult nature.

"If only I had not created the monster—I would have remained in blissful ignorance of that nature to the end of my days, I suppose. —There were the rooftops of Cambridge and the idyllic looking college with its green lawns in the distance. In the street below people were going to and fro between the shops and stalls. The smell of rotting fish came up distinctly, slops in the gutters, the smell of blood from the butchers across the way and rotten heaps beside the vegetable stall. I tried to imagine him climbing down upon the ledges and bay windows, a naked mistake of impossible proportions and ungainliness with bright yellow hair. I did not once think of how he was to be helped, but of how others might see him and hasten away in terror. Or did he wait until full night to creep about the city, perhaps on his knees. Who can tell, I thought, how he was able to come to grips with his body and move? A newborn is not given a body that can make its way around, such as I had given to him. A baby is granted that divine boon, a mother, to care for and help it adjust to its body and the world."

"— Something you said, Victor, a minute ago."

His gaze met mine swiftly and I saw in it again how shattered he was. The sky was beginning to pale and I knew he needed rest. I did. My judgment concerning him had moved to and fro, alternating between sympathetic patience and irritated haste over his deep, and what I thought at times, worthless introspection. We needed that rest he had spoken of, but I felt compunction to remind him of the catechism. Sometimes these things are wrong in their timing or motivation. Sometimes such qualms are right. It's not always easy to tell the difference between *intuitively right*, false piety, or a well-meaning but misplaced urge. It did not occur to me to study my compunction.

"You speak of how much you are suffering over yourself. What about grace?"

"Yes, I learned all that at my mother's knee," he said. "Enlightenment has almost done away with it. Or so I thought: in the Middle Ages Doctor Faustus was damned, with the advent of science he is redeemed. But I think not. Abner, what good does it do me to know about grace? I *need* grace, not doctrine about it. I need redemption, not instruction. I have no faith; does that exclude me, or are grace and redemption true? I know myself: In me they are not. I am overwhelmed with myself. And what of that creature out there? I built and tried to infuse him with life, but, as I live, that life was not mine. Where did it come from? I'm telling you, it chose of itself to come. —After I invited it, and what am I to do now that —?"

He stopped.

Victor looked away, then he looked back. "I don't want to hurt your own faith, Abner. Not anymore would I hurt people's faith. To do so would be to claim knowledge I don't possess. The enlightened—[and here our Victor made a bitter wry face] they will tell you reason forbids faith. I say that such reasoning is itself a kind of faith.... The reasoning apparatus will itself shortly be dirt and worm-eaten. —Though the advance had been too late for me, I had hoped to have a part in changing things before it surely happened to me. —Oh, I am mocked!"

He sank back exhausted but murmured as though to himself, "Of course it *is* so that those who believe absurdities will commit atrocities, and it is so what ever their established form."

I could stand no more. Used up, I turned and made up my bed. "I'm going to sleep. Mayhap you will, Victor."

I judged the monster would do as Victor said and that we would need no watch while he "waited." But as I lay down it occurred to me that the watch would be the monster himself. I heard Victor's sleep-breathing long before I myself fell deeply under the kindly spell.

These pretty Babes with hand in hand
Went wandering up and down;
But never more they saw the Man
Approaching from the town.

The lyrics and tune of the ballad found my mind as I slept and I awoke uneasy without knowing why. Then it came to me and I started up looking wildly thither and yon. Above and below the woods were full of bold light, not the soothing gold of morning, but the brilliant day of that white fire, the sun. There was a faint lingering smell of skunk which could have come from anywhere, but there was no sign of the monster, nor stir of any living thing.

I sank back and stared into the twigs and needled boughs above away from that portion where bright Helios stood. I fell to thinking of the myth and the youth Phaëthon's climb to the Sun's palace where Helios readily confirmed his fatherhood of this young man. In this story the Sun foolishly gave promise to anything Phaëthon would ask in token of his sonship. Perhaps his skill at fatherhood was not so great as his ability to handle the steeds of his burning chariot, for instantly he regretted the promise but kept it anyway. *Which is better*, I thought, *to break your word or allow such foolishness —a mortal boy to drive the fiery chariot of the god?!*

Seeing a poetic likeness to Victor's predicament in the figure, I looked toward him in the fir-shelter to ask his opinion were he awake.

Victor was gone. I jumped up in earnest and looked about again. "*Victor! Victor Besiegt!*" I stood foolishly calling. I stopped, and shook my head, sorry over my folly. Of course I had not considered the possibility that Victor had plans, and the monster had plans, and none to do with me in their original conception.

I did not make up the fire but took up my bedroll, gear and pouch of dried meat to eat on the way. I started off looking for signs of his passing.

Storyteller

"I need an Indian." This thought entered my head as, late in the day, disgusted, I was ready to give over searching through the woods. Victor would have to stay lost or be torn apart and gobbled up if it were left for my skill to track him. I hadn't learned much that was good about the Indians from my ignorant elders, but in my benighted bigotry I did grasp the fact of their woods wisdom. Abenaki natives, like their brethren in the New World had developed their culture and understanding from where they lived, whether plains, desert scrub, tundra, or woodland.

While we in the Old World sought to develop our surroundings to our comfort, need, and desire (and that to its detriment), they were content with the reverse in a greater harmony. They did not, however, extend this to the attuning of themselves with their neighbors. Thus the Abenaki needed confederation in order to protect them in their lands from the Iroquois to the west. Each, what you would call nation, fought, kidnapped, destroyed—the array of man's sin against his brother was in them as in ourselves.

It was as Jasper Mary said of us: "The hardy pioneers of Farmingham Royal, as they first named the town, looked down upon the natives both literally and figuratively—deeming them shiftless, childlike and slothful in comparison to their own rigorous, high-minded, provident Yankee and Puritan descent." We did not see the wisdom in knowing nature's uncultivated larder intimately and so well as to get a living of everything in it; or to make our way through it unencumbered, to our good and that of our family and community. At that time in Gott'im we took care of our paupers either last or—for those better attuned—at one's own table. The Abenaki gave the *first* of the hunt or gatherings to those least able in the community.

When I could not find the traces of Victor or the monster, I sat down at last, very low, and the sun was now low, cut off by the haunch of the mountain. Dusk hung about the woodland.

A voice spoke from the other side of the rugged tree I leaned against. "I am here."

The thrill went up my backbone and into my scalp and I sat up.

"What?" I said it cautiously.

"I here."

Then I recognized the speaking as womanish and Abenaki; a sign meant not to put the fright into me, but to signify her presence.

"Jasper Mary?" I asked it sitting still in the crooks.

"I have story for you," she said.

Here would be the right place to tell you about Jasper Mary.

By-the-by, I have seen her in heaven. She visits that part I dwell in and I have seen her in hers. They are not all that dissimilar, very bright and green, but the customs are different ... harmonically various (vastly), and each is mysterious to the other. She still spends time on Jasper Mountain, even into what you'd call the future. Every year she drops down to visit the village parade made in her honor. There is always an "Indian Princess" child elected to play the part of Jasper Mary on a pony, and although such trappings are not historical, the historic namesake still feels her honor deeply.

It occurs to me that you, neighbor, may scorn my tale for its insistence on this unlikely happenstance. I need an Indian and an Indian appears. But I did not know I needed one, truly. I was speaking rhetorically, irritably, and hardly aware. I had even forgotten my so speaking until long afterward. A great deal of metaphysical study has been done on the unconscious since those frontier days. Even skeptical modernity and you postmodernists will acknowledge the possibility of a deeper and richer awareness than what was allowed in what you call the Enlightenment of the 17th and 18th centuries. We had our hands full then battling superstition. For the rest: If you believe in heaven you do not very well believe in happenstance. But I will leave theology out of it at this time. The reach of my tale is too extensive for that.

Jasper Mary was the local, or you would say regional, healer. She traveled the Arossagunticook, in the main, but I'd no knowledge of her true range in those days: down to the sea in season as a certainty, up to the City of Québec, as the spirit led; but it's not far fetched to suppose her voyaging, as she called it, the length and breadth of the District of Maine as it was then called. New Hampshire, where too the Arossagunticook flowed, was also her territory. But we knew little of it.

What we knew were her tales, handiwork (she made ash baskets and quill pouches), and her doctoring. There was also the rumor, in the locale, of her treasure. It held that Jasper Mary had a treasure, or had hidden a treasure, or knew where the precious gemstone crystals could be dug in quantity. No one knew for sure and no one knew where, but it was generally spoken of by those who did not know her well. In after years some folks thought they knew about where to find this treasure, and the legend clung stubbornly in the local popular imagination. In consequence the plot was bought and sold, inherited and leased many times: pits were dug, the area pitted with them.

But I must get back to the story of Gott'im's monster or you will give me up in disgust.

I said to her, "I haven't heard one for a time or two now. Not since I was young, mayhap. You'd come to her door with a basket of herbs and Aunt Anna would buy the whole, basket and all. ... Mother did not buy, if I recollect."

"Yes. You Abner Bartlett." She said this as though it had not just occurred to her. I was placed as a particular soul of Gott'im. There was to her speech a faint Frenchness as well as the (as the scholars call it) Algonquin brevity, leaving out some verbs, tenses, articles and such. Economical it was. Indians as a rule had no desire for trivial speaking. One might agree to anything you declared just to quiet you and avoid the trouble of making a real answer. This was not so of story-making, storytelling. She had a rich throaty voice, took her time over it, did it right. Being a failed poet, I would rouse under her spell and even, in later life, apply some of her technique to my piddling works.

"Jas'Mary," I said as patiently, even politely, as I could for I was worn out, "have you seen anybody hereabout? A story would be fine but not just now."

She spoke again and then I noticed a gentle snicking sound every so often as we sat talking it over. I'm not sure, but it seemed like we were bartering as we spoke back-and-forth, her on the north side and me on the south of the great tree, the sun sending a final shaft against my right cheek. I turned away from it and heard her say next, "Will tell when you have story."

"But there is a... a monster." I said, "You know what a monster is?" I thought I heard her laugh, something secret and light like the snicking sound coming from her side of the tree. "Indian know monster," she said. It made me stop a moment. Had I heard a sarcasm? Or did she know of whom I spoke? I could not be sure. The apparent stoicism of the native is often a blind, I think.

"He is exceeding tall, with long yellow hair," I said after a moment.

"Abner Bartlett have story."

She said nothing more though I entreated, and so I became silent as well. I did not invite her to proceed.

I heard the soft *snicking* betimes and then she spoke. "N'Jacques, him so big'n'strong. Giant-killer. No thing living, dead, him fear."

Now I was fit to be tied. Here she was giving me one of those broken down Jack tales that were old when Columbus sailed the ocean probably. Here was a native so full of wisdom and lore and *real* mythology such as only the Jesuits have taken the time to study, and she was wasting my time on a fool French or Irish character from the Old World countryside. It was like seeing a proud Dawnlander of the eastern woodlands wearing white man's clothes and singing Yankee Doodle Dandy. But I bore it.

"Gott'im man call N'Jacque master-smart, that one," she said in her throaty voice. "Heaven nor hell him scare."

When Jasper Mary said this I recalled that once it was said she put some wampum down on the table of a priest to pray her man out of Purgatory for her, and when he got done, she took it up again and started with thanks for the door. "Where do you go with that?" he said. "Your man will go back into Purgatory."

"He no dumb man. Not go back to bad place when once he gone from there." I guess she had her own enlightenment.

Snick snick. The light was about gone and the sound ceased. The woods were full of that kind of dark where all the limbs and trunks and twigs are black against the lingering dusk.

I'm not going to find Victor.

"One night N'Jacque fall sleep by mistake his head to south instead of north. Sun come him wake to find his head turned backwards. Look down see his butt. He jump up, start walk. N'Jacque tumble down. Now N'Jacque afraid."

I waited. Then I said, "I see the moral," though I was too worried to consider it beyond noting its foolishness. It was a sort of English tale transmogrified—what you see the Indians laughing over like children. "Now tell me if you can about the monster. Did you see the white man in rags?"

"Monster eat skunk."

I jumped up and stumbled over the roots to the other side of the tree. "Where is he! Can you tell me? Can you help me find the white man?"

Then I saw she was holding something in her lap, glimmering against her buckskin skirt. She had been making a small basket bottom, weaving the thin strips of ash, circling about the wider stays. In the shade of firs surrounding her was too dark to see much of the Abenaki herself, but for her eye-whites and teeth. She set the basket bottom aside and sat very still. She was as still as the air about us. My eyes had got used to the twilight as eyes in twilight are wont. I saw her belt of wampum, the beaded icons of her history and tales, some were light as shell of which they were made.

Yes, I tell you all this now, but then I could not think of it: Victor was uppermost in my being. All being went into that concern. I wondered if she would say at last he were torn to shreds somewhere like those squirrels and hare I'd seen. It occurred to me that she would not care to haste the telling if he were past all help. Remember, she's a mighty healer. If you know her you know that she would curse a place, a business concern, but not a child, woman, or a man. But if Victor were dead—what about the monster? What about Gottheim on the other side of the mountain? The smell of skunk, at least, would warn someone in his way, but what if that one were a child, an old lady with no powder, ball or firearm? I was distraught but she sat still, all peaceable, and brought out her pipe.

I stood there, watching, waiting, even trusting just a bit. And then a bit more: as the scent of sweet fern in the clay bowl wafted up, and the glowing color of the coals sank from yellow to red. What could I do but sit down beside her? She held out the pipe, ceremonially with both hands. I actually considered smoking for it would have rested me, but then thought the better of it. I had to find Victor as soon as may be.

"Sometime we see white skunk," she said. "Every skunk white to begin. A trickster him. Like to be with Culuscap who made things, name all things."

"Yes," I said in spite of myself. "The white skunk begged the great hero to let him be his cook." I was remembering it as she had told me when a child. She told the children, even children of settlers, the stories of her folks... but not the grownups. Most Gott'im grownups scorned them. Not Aunt Anna or Mother. But even now—I was tempted to interpose that it was hard to conceive a skunk as cook. Who could eat a thing prepared by a critter like that?— Then I recollected that Skunk was not poisonous at that time. In fact, he was too lovely to be a cook!

"He was wanting to be with Culuscap when he did his great deeds. —Like the time Culuscap made the wolf a great dog-shaped rock for not cleaning up the Moose's guts that fell into the bay. Skunk wanted to *do* great deeds with Culuscap."

"Mm." Smoking, she nodded, pleased. "Him like the time Culuscap made Frog cough up water Frog stole from all earth. Frog a giant then—no more." She nodded again and went on. "Let Abner Bartlett tell how Skunk change to black and white."

"Will you say then what happened to the white man?... If the monster is... anywhere?" I could not help slipping back into my impatient concerns.

She smiled a bit. "Abner Bartlett not to barter for thought of Jasper Mary."

I hung my head, defeated.

I raised my eyes and said, "His fur was like a woman's silk, and white as fleece. He did not behave for Culuscap, despite his promise to be good when they went out to visit the Day Eagle. Instead, Skunk on impulse ran ahead and tied up Eagle's wings. Suddenly day was night. Culuscap came up and saw the eagle bound. He could get only one wing untied before the great bird flew on. Flew on but *one wing!* The day returned but always followed by the night and never any freer: The daylight had to yield, in cycle, to darkness each day after this.

"Culuscap was so mad he took the ashes from his stinking pipe and spoiled the pretty white fur. The awful smell came up from that—and Skunk was now pure black. But then, just as Skunk took off crying for his miserable pride, Culuscap—was it in mercy?— reached out a single finger and wiped a streak clean down his back, leaving him with but a touch of his former beauty."

I completed the story and looked back down at her, for my gaze had climbed up in pure abstraction as I spoke, lingering in the branches and among the faint first show of stars. I was exhilarated!

Her eyes maybe smiled. "You say moral."

I smiled back. "Skunk can't get away with tricking his Maker."

"Nay, nay. For this time the moral—man listen to story in time of trouble him blessed."

I looked at her with profound gratitude though it was almost too dark for seeing.

These stories are older than hills and mountains, I guess. The trick is to keep the telling fresh. Originality is a deceptive modern construction: imitation being the true art form. Tales seem to come out of our experience but I wonder if Plato isn't right that they existed before. This is what my studies seem to show me. The tales are kept in the archives of heaven. I have visited there often. All the learning of the tales in our persons is there, too, for us to recur to verbally; but thanks be to God we need never *live* them again when gone from the realm of suffering and sin.

Our mistakes are come again and again as each generation clothes them afresh in their youthful powers and the powers of the age. In the time of Gott'im's monster, and through my friendship with Victor, I came to understand that the limits of free will are the same as the limits of our power. Otherwise, in our sinful condition, we would say to God, "Give us more power that we might do yet more that we please."

In the day of Gott'im's monster our standard was modest: tradition. The disapproval of Gottheim kept our lusts checked. We had not yet thought to apply the fresh tenants of fledgling democracy to our individual lives: never for the purpose of license. The tradition of neighborliness was too strong in us for that. Our story was simple and local and told again and again; in gossip proving the force of one's repute. We cared for our neighbors' good opinion. Yet, though there was vanity and pride mixed in with that, the overall outcome was sound enough to prove a help among neighbors. We recognized our duties to one another.

Jasper Mary made me sit there a while longer answering a riddle or two (or three). It was well into dark when I found myself fortified by the storytelling for what lay ahead, and on my way back toward somewhat cultivated lands below the knees of the mountain: toward a rustic outlying hamlet of but four or five houses, and the meeting house and school, central for outlying steads. All I had learned from her riddles was that I should come this way if I wanted to be of any use whatsoever to Gottheim.

It took all night and part of the next day, under the big trees, over blowdown, and through the trackless snares of the puckerbrush, over territory you travel in about thirty-five minutes with skis or bicycles clamped on your automobile; or (if you are working), the pulpwood or trunks of white pine in your logging trucks. And I had to stop and rest and eat what handfuls were left to me from the smoke-dried meat I'd made on the mountain. Fortunately the weather was mild both night and day.

On that journey I tried to recollect each detail of Victor's telling. My mind, when not troubled by the monster's brute and bizarre appearance, turned over the homely story of his family and friends, loved ones ignored in the natural philosopher's pursuit of his own creation. Then the name of Clairson came back to me, and that fancied face of Victor's fiancée. But what I could not imagine was the galvanism of such passion for what I had seen in that awful creature: the only thing I could compare it to was my desire for recognition of poetic gift and work. I thought with a shiver if there were anything comparable in them... but laughed at myself: my poor poems were not armed to destroy the village or darken a household with blood.

After my death and spiritual rebirth I saw Henry Clairson. He told me of his own death at the hands of Victor's monster. I will tell you now, for this part does not come into Asa's telling, or the Gottheim local history written by Dr. Kimball using my journal, the accounts of others, and Loomis's notes.

At that time I did not know the sources of Victor's distress. Yes, I did hear him speak of the monster. But this was as I watched him through his illness. I had come back as promised and found him quite ill among the wrack of his laboratory. Mistakenly, I thought he had torn the place apart himself in a fit, or perhaps a delirium.

Clairson "spoke" in his light treble—I won't say "voice." In Henry Clairson's own transfigured face and shining-light eyes was the clear evidence of his transparent spirit, pure, compassionate, deeply loving. Clairson and I stood among the clouds above the earth, clouds suffused with light and mist. We were caught up together in the story of Gott'im's monster; yet all about us the clouds, full of peace and light, shone at whiles with loving faces looking downward, in wonder and in love, at what concerned *them*, gazing at the earth with its continuing and harrowing story. But the faces in these *clouds of witness* came in and out of focus, as we two were caught up in the story of our own time and place: as though the cloud and mist washed out these presences to our awareness, in the abstraction of our communion over this single story. Here in the lower heaven we are silent, as silent as the ocean of others who have come from the four corners to this vantage to gaze at whiles upon the Story of Earth. The story we are telling one another, in this shared communion, is made known, not through the elaborate mediums of voice-box, air and ear as 'twould be on earth, but directly, mind to mind.

I could scarcely believe this change in Victor. It was as though something had taken hold of the soul of the young man who had been praised to me by his professors, he with whom I had spent many happy hours studying both foreign and antiquated languages. Could this ill and bewildered youth be the same who had been, when last I knew, so happy in the College, in his studies, in the promise of his marriage?

He stayed with me, I had a nurse and doctor to visit him in my Cambridge rooms just off the Square, but for long it seemed he was out of his wits. At times he spoke as if a monster had seized him, were strangling him. (I did not know he had made a monster, that there could possibly be any such making—let alone by my friend.) Elsewise he jabbered of his own unfitness for life, the world which must surely abhor him. But he recovered, and we took up our studies together again, quietly. Peace took hold on my little household while his lay in shambles, for a time forgotten.

We had lively discussions on the contrasting qualities we found in the various mythologies incumbent upon the old languages. Perhaps owing to his scientific bent, he took the position that the stories he enjoyed were actually parasites on pure functional language; while I took delight in taking the measure of the language—that is its sounding—by what its heroes were doing. Even the difference in script, I said, shows forth great difference between the more delicate, sensitive, flowing stories and language of the Orientals; the Arabic or Persian: as opposed to the rigors of the northern and western poetry and tongues.

I, Henry, liked the hapless heroes best. Those who felt they were not in control of their destinies. Yes, Victor said, the orthography, the very shapes of the symbols with their corresponding sounds tell a large difference in temperamental qualities. Would the Persians, I wonder, be as concerned as we are with the conquest of nature?

I said, By their history, however, and if we look at the regimentation of their art…. But I looked at him a bit uneasily hearing that, hoping he were not harking back to the former thoughts of his illness. I need not have worried about that: though something horribly precipitous was coming. Victor was at ease again.

I think that the sunlight in my rooms, our fellowship and studies together, and the little comforts of life, perhaps convinced him of an escape from his destiny. He must have thought that, hearing no hue and cry, the monster had come to some sort of end —I cannot say what he may have hoped, perhaps drowning in the Charles? —and that he was never more to be troubled. Is not that like us, Abner, in our fallen state, earthbound and benighted? So easily do we let loose the notion, when a little time passes and nothing bad happens, that our actions will have no redounding?

It happened like this. Victor assured me he was well, and happy to be going back to his rooms, to tidy them up and set up housekeeping anew, in hopes of refreshing his studies, obtaining yet another degree, and sending for Regina. His hope now was in a professorship. I saw him but once again in that life.

When, after one other visit with him in his rooms, I heard nothing, and did not meet him again in the buildings or on the grounds of the college, I sent word to him: an invitation to join me in the partly wooded common of the River Park. I had planned an outing upon the Charles for us. He was to come but then came a message that he had gone back to Gottheim. Disappointed, I kept the engagement myself and took a punt on my own. Standing on the rear platform I pushed off with my pole toward the current.

The scent of water refreshed me, and I thought again, as I sometimes do on the river, of those words in Job: "Yet through the scent of water it will bud and bring forth boughs like a plant." Many is the time I set my quill pen scratching in some letter or other over the joys of punting on the river. Alternately poling or happily drifting, one stands almost as though walking amid the elements of water and air, relishing the blue sky, hung as far as the eye can see with white clouds, their dark bottoms trailing shadows over the countryside. The deep calming serenity, which I love so well in written poetry and Oriental myths, here plays its full range upon the entire being, drawing the susceptible soul deeper into beauty. I have no complaint: it's true there was a deep and contrasting horror which came to me there on the river among thoughts uplifted by nature, but one can ask no better than to be doing what one loves when met by man's last great enemy, death.

I did not know but what I had struck a rock. But I was surprised in the undue violence of the collision. Then I was under the water, the shadow of the overturned craft above me blocking the glooming rays of the sun beyond. His great hands were already about my throat; his scarred and hideous face, grimacing with violent power, all before me. His hair was spread like an open fishing net. I had never in life spent myself as I did in those moments under the dark water, but to no avail. Those mighty hands harrowing me among the deeps, that frightening suffocating power... it unlocked me from my earthly being and I drifted out, away.

.... Now all was peaceful. On the opposite shore, in the glimmering trees stood one I had always hoped to see. I was with and knew him. He knew me. He showed me his hands and feet, his side. He was bright, burning almost, with love. I knew then all the love I missed in life, mostly without ever knowing it. Yet there was deep familiarity in it, too, for I recognized then the shadow of earth that had somehow always kept me quite from that light of all eternity, while never wholly blocking it. It shone as it had from the beginning... but now the shadow was gone.

He gestured toward the river, and though longing still to look on Him, I felt too that I wanted to obey His every thought for me, and so I looked. There was the monster of Victor's making, and I knew for a certainty Victor __had__ made him, and that he was deeply repentant but still must live with the consequence of... of that creature there bobbing like some ugly Leviathan ...and now turning against the current toward the opposite shore, leaving my hapless body for the fish to feed upon: swimming toward what I thought must still be Charlestown where rose Bunker Hill with Joseph Warren's wooden pillar, the urn atop it glinting. That shore was across the impossible divide, from where no man may come save he has been called hither by our Lord, however untimely seeming.

One of Jasper Mary's riddles set me thinking. It involved both the making of the Native community and the woodland that Culuscap had set it in. Culuscap naturally had a hand in making all the creatures and forming the land. And while this was still going on, he would visit his various native communities, the people he loved, and to whom he tried to show wisdom. The riddle asked, "What turned the water of the land from thin to thick, but now from thin to thin to thick?"

I'd judged of course that, it being Jasper Mary telling the riddle, part of the answer would involve Culuscap. So I had blithely answered *Culuscap.*

"Abner not get to Victor so easy."

But this response had made me easier: she was admitting Victor and that he lived. I rooted around my memory and came up with the tale of Culuscap finding the people so lazy with the goodness of the syrup falling straight into their mouths —from the tips of the twigs during the thaw: all they were good for was lying beneath the trees all day long getting fat. So he re-created the sugar maple just enough to make it flow only with a watery sap in that season. After that the people really had to work to make that sap yield its sweet. (He did the same with the birch tree but made it require twice as much effort.) Maple trees turn the water of earth and sky into sap, and men and women in Gott'im turn it into syrup in a sugaring off house.

Jasper Mary, I believe, understood that the riddles would keep my mind busy. It was in sore need of such occupation, helping to keep the fear at bay. I'll not tell you now how I pieced the others together to bring me to this exact hamlet; but here I found myself on the shoals of evening, and set about, secretly, trying to discover where the nearest sugarhouse stood.

As I have said, it was one of our long cold Maine springs, but sugaring off was already done for the year, and I knew that house would be empty. Probably no one would visit there again except by happenstance until the following year. I pondered that it would indeed make a good hideout for someone in the fix Victor found for himself, providing it were remote enough. Someone who had just been nursed back to health by an admiring acquaintance, and now felt no compunction to.... Was I getting away with myself? — Probably.

I thought, *If you are going to be angered, you are going to be of no use.* And: Remember, you still have no understanding of what happened or why. A common sense can go a long way toward keeping you from trouble. After all, he did leave me my lousy blanket and go off in his tatters. But —

Where is the monster?

I had been following the clues from the riddles, but could not help thinking now as I stared off downslope toward the hamlet in twilight. It huddled deep under ledge that soared above out of sight in the puckerbrush where trees clung to sheer sides and among fallen rocks. In fact, I was still uncertain: had I indeed come to the right place?

It may be hard in your land and language to remember just how fearsome the woods could be for the unwary. But there was great beauty in their deeps as well. Poetry and mystery dwelt there side-by-side with hardship: a hardscrabble life was all you could have here in that time. There are now no more trees of that size in the mountains of Western Maine, or in Maine for that matter. Except for bold coast resorts and fishing grounds, and blueberry barren downeast, this is a state largely owned by paper company interests, an industrial woodland of far thinner trees. On the other hand, because it is so, there are still woods for the creatures to inhabit, woods for the huntsman, those who would gather the sap in spring, and those who would live more remotely.

What I was looking at as I stood there under the eaves gazing down on the hamlet moved my soul. It seemed *dear*. It must have been the juxtaposition of the life one has to live here, and the unfathomable beauty in which it is lived. The hamlet was steeped in twilight shadow, whitewashed hewn log houses bravely proclaiming themselves, cows in the dooryard being milked, cellar foundations holding the last of the old season's produce and the small barn its hard-won provender. Here and there a faint light showed within. Then a man's voice drifted out into silence from some yard, and a woman's answered from within. A dog barked.

I do know him. He brings a cartload of apples to Gott'im every fall... and meat. One of the Sessions, a meatman (what we used to call the hunters who brought in game for those who couldn't get it themselves).... And maple syrup in the spring he brings to Capt. Melville's store.

I looked back up the slope behind me and knew that his sugarhouse must be up where those bare limbs bristled in the pall of last light, away from the dark clump of white pine hard by. I turned back and quietly made my way until I struck a path leading back down to the dooryard. But now I went up toward the grove.

Now that I knew where I was going, the worrisome thoughts thronged my mind again. Was Victor chasing the monster to kill him, as he had said? Or was the monster chasing Victor? As seemed more likely. The monster is a he, but is he a man? Is this a human being? Does he think, have a soul. If so where did it come from? How did he learn anything with no one to teach him? Can he speak?

The Monster Speaks

Should I be going to Gottheim to alert the village that a monster is loose? Would they think I was woods queer? Should I go over to home and get the firearm, come back and kill it; or go alert them, then come back and try? Will they just think I'm crazy? *Abner*, I told myself, *you don't even know if he's here.* Try to find something out before turning yourself into an unfettered cannon.

I climbed up into the sugar bush, now going as softly as I could, applying all my craft to make no sound. Dark came on and the path was not well-worn as it might have been earlier in the season: The winds of spring had knocked down the loose dead branches and twigs. Sinews of my being grew tauter with every step in trying to avoid them. I was straining to move both swiftly and quietly as may be, and to listen for any sound. These woods were not familiar to me.

Then I heard it, a remote murmur. I stopped to listen. Dark had come down, but I could see the black squared shape in among the trees. I moved closer, and heard the voice speaking. Placing my footfalls with great care, straining everything in me, I moved softly forward and stopped again. Now the voice was more distinct, a voice different in quality from any voice I had heard before.

The thrill shot up my spine. I stood unmoving. He spoke English with a strange accent, certainly nothing I'd ever heard before and could not imagine it from my reading about other languages. It was not fluid speech. The voice was deep, highly suggestive of power, somewhat thick, rich, and reckless. I could imagine it making brutal deafening noises. As it came through the trees I knew I would have to draw closer, in order to understand what it was saying; and try to understand what all was there, how they were placed, how I was placed to deal with it. But I was afraid. The smell of him, the smell of skunk, was here.

As I had moment to moment since first seeing the monster, I prayed. A wordless wild arrow up through the dark naked trees.

Then I moved closer. It took awhile to get near enough the long side of the little sugarhouse to catch distinct speech. One of the hinged hanging shutters was propped a little and that was where the following conversation, not quite whole, came out to me. The stench was stronger. I stood against the great bole of a sugar maple, receiving the faint scent of the tree's rough living hide, leaning into it with strange gratitude and a furtive rest, hopeful also that the shade of its strong side would hide me. Then I heard the striking of flint, and after a bit a faint glow seeped under the shutter, as though someone had lit and shaded a lamp. This made me a little easier for their eyes would adjust, making it harder to descry me should one of them step out unexpectedly into the dark.

I never found out how Jasper Mary knew to send me here (she was killed not long after this by thieves). I thought, perhaps she overheard them planning...? Nor did I understand how it worked out that I came in good time to hear this exchange between Victor and his creation: Oddly, it seemed their colloquy had just begun. How had things come together just so?

"Yes. This is the good thing done for you. My maker. My maker. More than was done for your little one. No name. You gave me no name. You told me nothing. You ran away. But I will tell you what I will do, your creation, the monster you call me. You gave me no help, but I give you help: I spare your other friends. I tell you what I will do."

"*Wait!* What do you mean? My other friends? Those in the Village? What do you mean by *other*?"

"Clairson."

"What do you mean, Clairson? What do you know about Henry? — He disappeared." Victor's voice had been full of alarm (an emotion I had not heard him express before), but suddenly on that last phrase it dropped. Then something sickening was said in a murmur almost inaudible to me. "Indeed, you *would* have killed Abner, had I not followed you here."

There was silence. Then came a noise, a sort of scraping, as though something moved over the packed dirt floor. "Tell me!"

"Not now."

Again the silence.

"How did you learn to talk? How have you come to do what you do?"

In these words I sensed the scientist, the maker in Victor, stirring inquisitively.

"My friends. Where I lived, where I learned about Clairson."

Impatiently, "Friends?! Tell me."

"The monster can have no friends?—Your house, my maker."

"You lived in my house? —You never left?"

"In the cellar."

"— Your friends?"

"Mother Griswold."

"The landlady? How? She would not befriend such—"

Was it answered mockingly, with bitterness, scorn? "—Such baby monster."

What a voice! But a voice of so little help to its expression. So much brutal emotion!

"She'd be afraid!"

"Yes. Monster would scare Mother Griswold. She befriended, your word, without knowing. I was in the cellar, got my food from Mother Griswold, learned all of Mother Griswold and her brother, daughter, little one. At night I helped them. I cleaned the yard, repaired the wall, stacked wood. Mrs. Griswold did not like to: I wrung the chickens' neck. I did well: they would not hear it. I think it was love. Love. What they say, love."

After seeing the monster kill with his mouth and begin eating the white skunk; hearing this, about loving them, frightened me almost as much as anything else I overheard while they were in the sugarhouse.

"The cellar is mine. I hide there, no one goes where it's dark. If she came for carrots or potatoes, rutabagas, I hid in the coal cellar. If they came to the coal cellar I hid with the roots. I ate the old roots and the mice and rats, not the cats, they liked cats, went back to your chamber and found clothes to wear, clothes of my maker."

"I don't think they'd fit. Those aren't my clothes."

"These are from Gott'im."

"What?—from some clothesline? —I don't understand how no one has seen you."

"They saw monster near your house, the college. Not long. I came back to your house, they were scared. Their fear makes me hide. I was scared of their fear."

"Yes, so you hid in the cellar and stole food from Mrs. Griswold's kitchen. Or the ashcan, perhaps? How did you learn to speak?"

Silence was in the sugarhouse.

Victor urged more speech. "What about the others? Her daughter and so forth?"

"They taught the baby, the monster learned too. A child."

"Yes. I remember the child."

Still leaning into the maple tree, I thought, *You barely remembered that child, Victor.*

"A child had those who made it teach it. I know: another one was coming, a child. I had a hole, I heard them and watched them. They loved."

Impatiently, "So they spoke of many things then, taught the child, you learned. But what about Clairson?"

"They spoke of you. Told me your name, all about Victor Besiegt. Victor was ill with Clairson."

"Tell me!"

"Not now."

Again there was silence, followed by more scraping. I also heard something that sounded like the munching or crunching of nuts, perhaps even a creature, small creature with bones. Even from here the lingering smell of the white skunk was awful: At times I heard Victor gagging.

Irritable, he said something I missed. I heard someone walk restively about in the little house. Perhaps a circuit of the stove on which evaporation earlier had taken place. The tread was lighter than what would have been the monster's. The monster does not speak with cunning: That is, there was no quality of it in his speech. But I think he conversed with cunning nonetheless. Victor became increasingly restive and anxious, I judge. It was that "not now," which pitched the unease into both him and myself. Remember, I did not yet know what had happened to Clairson. I judged Victor had suspected something before now, however.

It was much later in the ordeal of the monster that Victor told me the conversation he had had with Mrs. Griswold upon his return to the rooms following his illness. He reported this to me while we stood guard outside his fiancée's house. At that time he filled me in on a number of details, trials, and fears.

Apparently Mrs. Griswold was an excellent gossip, and this accounts for much that the monster learned about his maker; indeed, everything he learned at that time. Perhaps because he was so secretive, the doings of one Victor Besiegt were speculated upon again and again in the kitchen (behind the undertaking parlor), between the loving intimates of the house, Mrs. Griswold: her brother, her daughter and son-in-law; even other tenants and the help. Yet, for all that gossip, they never knew what Victor was about up there in the upper chamber of their establishment and apartment house. The household, of course, was not without knowledge of the attack upon their house by storm. But they knew nothing of Victor's running away, and evidently had no knowledge that the topmost chamber was ransacked by the monster in his throes to gain the mastery of his being and surroundings: The storm had been local, violent and percussive. It had blown open shutters and doors. Victor did not correct their view of things when he came back to set the place to rights.

The talk inside had ceased. I thought vaguely how strange it all was, Victor Besiegt the schoolmaster and eminent scientist being in there with his monster having a conversation. I found I was leaning hard against the maple, my arms hanging limp along its sides, my cheek pressed against the bark. Though aching and still burthened with my bedroll and belongings, I dared not move. The night had acquired an air of vagueness and unreality. I felt weary and a bit numb. Silence, scattered with small noises, deepened.

Oo-oo—oo-oo. In my sleep I hear the hooting of an owl and, not rousing, thought of the owl's ear. Dr. Kimball pointed this out to me from one of his stuffed specimens: The ear on its right side is shaped differently from that of its left, helping the owl to pinpoint its prey, with triangulation, *precisely* in the complete dark. Would you think you could put something over on a God who thought up a creature like that? —But Victor would say I had better read up on my Erasmus Darwin.

I heard the owl again and started wide awake, clinging to the rough tree to steady myself, still in the midst of the nightmare. So alert was I that my hackles felt raised like the quills of a porcupine. Light still seeped, and some small knocking noises, from under the shutter. The monster said, "You shake. I make the fire."

"You better be careful. That smoke on the wind. You don't want the man to come." Victor's voice was tremulous with the chill. Or was it nerves? Instantly I thought of his tatters and realized that he was in a bad way again after a stressful night and day of traveling and wrestling with the... being.

Oh God!— The quills upended again as the monster made a horrible noise, oddly metallic. I will not try further to describe — no I could not, if I had all the poetic powers—of a Blake or a Samuel Taylor Coleridge—in the world. The dogs far below were barking.

I heard him say, in the most brutish horrible way, "Maker now to teach his monster!? Maker to have his monster do that or this!?"

A huge smell of the skunk came out the door from his breath. His scream was metallic like a panther's—what you might call a mountain lion, which we still had plenty of in those days. He growled out low like a bear: "I'll kill man! He come near I'll kill! No one will stop monster! Victor Besiegt!"

I shook like a popple leaf in a storm, and the next thing I knew Victor had stumbled out and lay half in, half out of a patch of light from the doorway. And not far from my tree. I did not know but what the monster had felled him. Without thinking I knelt, still holding onto the tree, and stretched out to touch his arm that lay in shadow. I gripped it, and he turned his head toward me. He was shaking, I could see nothing of his features. I withdrew behind the tree.

Victor stood with surprising quickness given his condition and said huskily, trembling, "I won't leave. I'm coming back to be with you." He set his hand to the door frame to steady himself and moved in, shutting it and putting the latch on. This all happened very fast, and the monster had not moved, that I could tell, to bring him back. I think he would have gone after Dr. Besiegt had he tried to get away. But Victor had gained courage through the mere touch, the clasping of my hand on his arm; and in knowing that I was there, a witness. He did not want his creation to know of my presence. I'm certain this saved my life.

Who can tell why we are born into the world? Back then, if we thought about it, we common folk in the New World believed that it was for the glory and pleasure of God. And for this reason many never thought of that *why* at all (unless something happened to them). We attributed everything evil to the fallen nature of mankind; strangely, rarely questioning how evil could even be, since we also believed that God made everything and God is good. The Enlightenment, of course, was busily picking these beliefs apart, but here in woodland Gott'im we still believed such things, even if acting contrariwise. Yet all thoughts of this kind are merely abstractions. When we think concretely, we know we have actually to *do* something in this life. And what I had been *doing* was transforming myself into a grownup.

Are children born into the world to learn its laws? We learn about gravity by dropping our toys and watching the grownups stoop to pick them up for us. I am one of those people with a great memory, especially of early life. I remember sucking on a rag doll, dropping it and, me still in her arms, watching my mother retrieve it for me. We would do this several times until she got tired of stooping while holding me and put the doll away. I did not easily tire of such games. I did not call it gravity, of course, but I knew it was there, invisibly.

We were a numerous family, and sometimes I tested gravity in the arms of my elder sister, Philippa. Once I received a nasty bump on the head while playing the game of "faint and catch." We were both older then, and it was a delight to play this game, in which I would fall backwards with a kind of sigh, and she would catch me before I hit the ground. I showed a deep trust in her and an understanding of the law, but these laws are rather impersonal, and unforgiving. She was conversing in the schoolyard with a friend in the midst of our game, and had turned from me, while I, unaware, dropped back with a sigh and collided heavily with the ground.

This thought that children are put into the world to learn its laws came from Philippa. Philippa had married a Holt and was raising a numerous family of her own in Gott'im while I was out in the wilderness on Jasper Mountain trying to understand what I was meant to do. Not what I was meant to be—that is a more modern construction. To be? What is being? ...My whole being then was going into helping Victor deal with this monster. She was, especially, one of the numerous reasons why I longed to divert the monster, to kill the monster, whatever need be to protect the village and environs of Gottheim.

Before I left— and she knew what I was about— we sat at her kitchen table, the door snugly closed, dim rainy light streaming in the small window. She was braiding a rug from scraps, but then she stood to pace at the spinning in the corner. The pot of stew from scrapings of the bottom of the barrel, scant carrots and potatoes from the cellar, onions and herbs from the rafters upstairs, was hanging in the hearth. There was a rich fragrance in that room then. Had I not been turned to such a pitch in this trouble I would have remembered that heavenly smell with longing. My nieces and nephews and her stepchildren were on the floor everywhere, or coming down the ladder, or in and out from the next room; reading or playing on that rainy day.

Philippa said, "And not only that, but one of the laws they learn is that parents are meant for the teachers of some of these laws (having learned them first as children themselves). Is there any other purpose, real and goodly purpose, in this life Abner? Yes, I believe it. But I cannot impart it, only tell you what I have learned."

"But I feel the need for so much more. I *was* going to be that poet. The desire has not left me now I have failed. At least I think it is a desire for that." I looked around at my little friends, the child on my lap; the one with its arms around her neck; recognizing great comfort in such friendship but feeling a dite stifled in that rainy day household, all the same.

"It's a chance to serve... like we are served by the Father... whose son was also obedient....We take care of one another."

Yes, the law of gravity is impersonal and unforgiving, but you have got to expect that of something with so much responsibility. It cannot look to left nor right when it has such a big job to do. As far as I know, gravity is what keeps the natural world, the entire cosmos, on course. It may be there are only two beings: God, the only supernatural; and, including the angelic laws, God's creation. The latter is incapable of containing him. It is also the natural. Even though I died long ago, I am still part of the natural order and continue to learn about it. We don't just sit up here playing harps, as some with lesser imaginations, especially those of my own century, might think.

And more is being revealed all the time. You, of course, know all about this, having witnessed the explosion of knowledge and its extravagant applications in your lifetime. Many of you already are and some of you will soon be learning, from those who study this kind of thing, that the super cluster of which earth is but a mote, afloat upon its current, seems to be flowing toward the dark something astronomers will be calling the Great Attractor. Visibility shows us much, but the invisible is the greater portion by far. You have only recently discovered this. What is unseen has a far greater gravitational influence than what is seen. You cannot see Dark Matter.... but what do you *know*? You know the *pull* of gravitation. Would not you think, just knowing what you know off the top of your head (as you say), that something is going on with this great law, seeing how it keeps such order? Think of how the galaxies and clusters—let alone the solar systems—of the Big Bang are held spinning, everything moving toward—? —A spectrum of visible and invisible color and form, moving with brilliant consistency, precision, and verve. And then there is that other thing, the abyss—you call it chaos—which we won't get into now.

From under the shutter propped ajar, I scarcely caught the words of Victor, speaking with a catch as though in grief. "Had I known you would kill Henry... had you approached me, I would have done what you wanted before now.... I would have done ... *even this* to stop it...."

That awful voice moved. "No you would have got Clairson away. Victor Besiegt would have run. I had to know where. I know Gott'im now. They call Gott'im. Because I kill him you know I will do that bad thing. If you do not make me my bride."

—Make another —? Another monster?! Again I clung, shuddering as the popple leaf might—. (In the slightest breath it would. Have you seen them shake when there seems no wind? Visibly shaking with the invisible?)

"You learned all this— from the Griswolds? You said something—. What happened to the Griswolds?"

I sensed Victor's desire to cease speaking of that other thing in these words. He must have been desperately thinking. Scrabbling about in his thoughts.

Here is the story in summary of the monster's time at the Griswold's:

I've told you how he learned of life in his hiding place. One day the monster espied his maker's arrival: Through one of his peepholes, the crack beneath the door, perhaps, from the cellar into the hall of the private residence he saw Dr. Besiegt. The monster was tall, and had other such holes in the wall along the dark stairwell that gave him access to other rooms. Have you ever noticed that the eye requires but a hole as small as a nailhead for its watch? As I listened to him tell of his time there, I found myself astonished at how rapidly he had gained his feet, command over his senses, his form, and cunning direction for his thought.

Forgive me: As you have seen me do before now, I cannot help but draw the likeness to the Industrial Revolution and its aftermath of burgeoning, what you might call, technocracy. Think of the long span of our primitive history, our periodic enlightenment, even our slow-moving renaissance. Thousands of years of it before Manchester England, Robert Fulton and precipitant industrial advance. You have come to understand that the developing systems of humankind have a life of their own. Transportation, information, education, medicine, commerce, trading, construction, military, the making and selling of all goods, political systems, governance, law. And more, so much more. In fact, your interconnecting systems are alive not only because their inventors were and are living, but because the living keep them going, much as the heart pumping, the nerves synapsing, the brain firing, the blood transporting messages; all keep the body alive. But what is the central authority, the commanding unit of heart, mind and conscience necessary to make the living system—a living creature—balanced, healthy, integrated— whole?

The monster's development was rapid through his vital intimate connection with the human beings in the Griswold's household. Even before Dr. Victor Besiegt's name was mentioned in the course of the conversation between Victor and the undertaker's wife, he had a sense that something was different, special, about the man he saw. His first glimpse of his maker's face came back to him with increasing clarity. He may even have experienced an intuition: He might have loved this man. There was a man in workman's clothes with Dr. Besiegt, and when, in the wee hours of that same night, the monster climbed to the upper chamber and looked in the window he saw the place orderly, clean and swept. He came to understand that they had been busy together that day working to set all to rights. Yes, this was his maker.

In the sugarhouse, the monster spent many words describing his thoughts and emotions on seeing his maker in Griswold's household. There was not hatred but a torrent of love and bemusement mingled with the torment of extreme attraction. The monster was far from repulsed, but he was not happy. And he had to stay hidden. There were hints enough of what waited in store for him should he appear.

You would call it an urban legend: Back then in Boston, while Victor was recuperating secluded at Clairson's, the monster had apparently been seen by only one person at a time, with a great production of fear in both the seeing and in the seen. He was legendary but ultimately unbelievable.... Until some of those who claimed to have seen him met to compare notes in a local tavern. But more on this later.

Henry Clairson came by to inquire after Victor. His creature's torment increased when he recognized their communion: This was his maker's close friend. Later he heard Victor tell the Griswolds that he must go to Gott'im to visit his prospective bride. From the Griswolds' conversation the monster learned that Gottheim was up the Arossagunticook in the mountains of Western Maine. When Victor left on this errand the monster's jealousy climbed to its pitch. Still he did not hate Victor. Remember, he knew *all* of domestic life. The thought of Victor having a bride was hard to bear, but it was recognizable, understandable and later, after much thought, even comforting to his creature.

In the archives of *US Historical and Current Newspapers* you will find a microform copy of the *Boston Mirror* account of that tavern meeting and the subsequent sighting of the monster entering the Griswold establishment. Under the heading of "Monster Sighted Roaming the Rooftops of Cambridge" ran the words:

Yesterday evening the incredible suddenly took on the mantle of credibility when a monster of astounding shape and proportions was observed by witnesses, outside the Griswold Undertaking Establishment, wringing the neck of a chicken before flinging and then climbing over the wall after it. Following a general hue and cry around this event, the household was roused and set to flight when the monster was spied climbing out the window of an upper chamber while the crowd looked on from below. Many were the witnesses, including one John E. Trowbridge of Water Street who said, 'I saw him jump the lane to the opposite rooftop, a big ungainly-seeming brute but with proven ability and power. His hair light-colored and flowing like a woman's, he climbed about, much as you have read in the travelers' tales who have seen the great apes in the Africas.' There are various accounts of sightings in other parts of the city since, some more or less credible, others not so.

This scene of dramatic sensation progressed after a meeting, occurring in the Shipmasters Tavern, of those who had earlier espied the monster in these streets of Cambridge and Boston. At this meeting were harmonized all previous accounts of this colossal being's physical form and behavior, in such precise manner as could not be ascribed to the taps of the ale served within....

The article continues with an account of the Griswolds' horror and revulsion over their discovery of the monster revealed.

For many months they had been accustomed to commenting on the good deeds done their household, which they ascribed to either one or another of its members, or some spritely and kindly friend without the premises. This was before it was revealed the true source of these deeds; none other than the malevolent shape of a monster, living beneath their very household for they knew not how long, at least many months. Just how it had come to be living there, they knew not, any more than they knew the source of its astonishing formation. None who have seen it can conceive of its having been granted the breath of life through such means as of the ordinary paths of conception and human issuance.

There are minutely detailed follow-up accounts in subsequent editions, but finally there is silence on the subject of this fantastic intrusion into city life. The monster had disappeared, never to forget the Griswolds' betrayal.

Within the sugarhouse he was saying, "It happened many days after I killed Clairson and then the chicken outside. All kindness and love toward them— gone. Clairson I did not know except he was maker's friend and I did not like that. But the Griswolds—! The Griswolds betrayed your monster. Yet I loved—could not kill them but let them flee. Then all sought me and wanted to kill. *I am a monster!*"

Again the monster shook the cold spring night with that agonizing metallic panther-scream. (The dogs far below in the hamlet began again to bark and howl. In the deep silence that followed I almost sensed his bewilderment, anguish—despair over his *being*. I had no thought but that; certainly not of there being a remedy for it, although his agony in this moment did recur to me later.) As it ended, my terror resumed with increase.

After a moment he said it with a calm that surprised me for its subtlety: "Dr. Besiegt will make me my bride."

Rather boldly, I thought, Victor said, "If I refuse."

Again, with that subtle calm, came the answer. "No bride for my maker."

Again there was silence, into which came the knowledge of Clairson's disappearance. With awful suddenness I understood why the monster was here on Jasper Mountain. Why he had been in secret to Gottheim. Why he had haunted Dr. Besiegt and myself. I understood what Victor's answer would mean, whether yea or nay. Either course was intolerable.

You are intolerable, a monster. Yes. I will kill you.

As I listened, straining, a part of my mind was already busy with his destruction. I had stopped trembling.

Then with sudden alacrity Victor said, "*I-will-do-it.*" I heard him say, "It will not be easy. It will take a long time, and you must be patient. But you must stand off. I will not work well with you staying nigh, troubling me."

There came a *chuffing* sound which, after a moment, suggested laughter to me. The monster may have laughed in mockery, remembering that Victor would indeed have run off with Clairson. He may have laughed in delight that he was to have his own bride. Without seeing his glance, I could not tell from its tone what this laughter might signify.

"How did you make me, maker? What am I made of?" Came the chuffing sound again.

Silence again, and I sensed Victor calculating. The air about me now was fragrant with wood smoke. Unlike Victor, I knew the size of the settlement down below and that any such scent would hold no alarm for the neighbors there at this time of night. In the light of day, with smoke drifting upward out of the distant trees, yes—alarm. But wood smoke-smell at night might have come from anyone's hearth unseen.

"You knew the undertaker's work?"

"He readied and buried the dead in the ground. I saw them, sometimes, at night. This is dead, I said. When I am like that I will no longer be. What will I be? How can I not be?"

I was astonished, and felt Victor must be too. *Silence.*

He continued. "I followed Arossagunticook into the wild District of Maine. I traveled at night and broke into cellars and got food and ate creatures in the woods. I slept by the pool-water lying smooth. I woke up and looked in. I was there, a picture of me. I stirred it with my finger. It broke and came back together again. I did not look like you, or anyone, but what I heard them say, brutish. Did you make me out of the dead, Victor Besiegt? Is that why these scars? The monster was dead first?"

"I put you together from what I found there, and in the morgues of the cities. I hadn't power enough to bring you to life and will answer no questions of that sort. ...But I may make another apparatus... maybe.... There is a secret to life, what ignites life—never mind."

Chuff-chuff. "Make my bride."

Bride for the Monster?

"Give me some of the acorn meat," I heard Victor say. "I'm exhausted and going to lie down here now, after this." He raised his voice a bit. "You move off a bit, while I sleep."

I knew this last was meant for me, too. I heard some moving around inside and decided to do as instructed.

I was stiff and cold. It took much for me to stifle oral expression of my complaint. Still cumbered about with my bedroll and pouches, I turned and picked my way carefully down through the woods, searching for a resting place not too far away. I knew the direction to Gott'im from here and situated myself to be out of line of sight but within hearing should they pass.

I tended to believe Victor —that he *had* been chasing the monster. But this was only an indication of how cunning the brute could be: he had lured Victor into the wilderness, exhausting him to the point of breakdown, and it seemed to me now that Victor had indeed thought the monster the quarry and not himself. Victor maybe had not misled me. In fact, however, they had been chasing one another like a dog after its own tail. I nestled into the deeply shadowed crooks of three great trees, and, to keep bats off me (possibly now coming out from hibernation and migration), pulled a blanket over my head. I thought, They *are* inseparable, almost like Siamese twins joined at the spine. At least one will *have* to die—most particularly the monster. —I hoped before there could be another monster.

But I did not sleep instantly. I was scratching and thinking of the old hermit's camp. Then my mind was busy with *this* monster, knowing he would probably leave the sugarhouse while his maker slept. He would not go far, fearing that even in his weakened state Besiegt might get away — get back to Gott'im with the alert. Now that he had extracted the promise, made very sure the necessity, he was going to stick close to Dr. Besiegt. But the thought of his wandering around, perhaps nearby, made me sleepless.

If I had known what lay in store for us in the next hundred years through the inspired application of the sciences, my mind might have been busy with that. At that time the only subway we in Gottheim had ever heard about was the underground walkway of Monticello, connecting the great house with the slave quarters. But within a few decades our quaint and creaking waterwheels powering the grist mills would be replaced by sprawling behemoths, paper mills of hellish qualities such as only a man could dream up.

Adam and Eve notwithstanding, I would have been convinced that if such as my sister, Philippa Holt, had been granted ambition, power and education enough, she would have made paper mills *from the start* to be things of beauty, proper scale and proportion, *and* practicality. There would have been no waste, no stench, no poisoning of the rivers....

The hideous form of the monster (yet somehow eliciting that mysterious appeal of beauty or magic), shows you what Victor was thinking of: he was driven by a single-minded passion to make a living creature, determined first upon that, future be damned, surroundings—who thought of that? Friends? Family? Who knows, maybe he thought to work in successive drafts (much as I was thinking of in that matter of poetry, soon to weigh on me again)? Is it not so? —inspiration and invention of science, these are not despicable except when poorly or wrongfully executed?

Aas I lay curled up in the hard roots, listening. Hiding beneath the trees, I tried to recall Victor's bride-to-be, Regina.

The more I spent time in this harrow, the more my memory of her increased. It seemed to me that she was the little angel of the Besiegt household following the death of the mother. I remembered paupers being welcomed at the kitchen table, the same meals the family had in the dining room and waited on by the same household helpers. This, I was sure, was her doing. And from a very young age. I also remembered her as nurse-mother to little Greenleaf. And that she was gentle and pretty with auburn hair, not the bright reddish silk that kids tended to make fun of, but wavy and heavy. She was a bit older, and, like a lot of the boys, I may have had a crush on her. Beyond that I did not recall much.

I was worried about Gottheim and my own family but the fulcrum of the monster's fixation was the Besiegt household. Likely harm coming to others nearby would be almost incidental, solely because they found themselves in the way. The Besiegt household was not in the village but up a lane off the road toward the hamlet of Twombly.

I had no idea how I could speak with Victor and tell him my intention of guarding the household while he went about his distraction of the monster. I thought he had made a mistake in insisting the monster keep away from him. Perhaps he would think better of it. I could not bring myself to believe that he would actually set up a laboratory somewhere to work on another monster: He would *feign* doing this, perhaps even gather all the materials needed into an isolated workshop somewhere far away. I felt a great need to talk with him, plot with him, and my mind turned to the sole firearm in the Bartlett household, my father's old Revolutionary War musket.

Then I smelled him. I had no other sense of him at first, but as the skunk smell increased I heard him moving about the woods above me.

Chuff chuff.

I heard his strange laughter.

"Abner will help Victor make the bride." The rich thick syllables came through the trees.

The monster was speaking to me.

A combination of thrill and revulsion sickened, body and soul. He was up in the woods, addressing himself directly to me in words of warning and instruction. I huddled very still in the crooks with the covers tight about me, unsure if he knew my exact location.

"Everything Victor tells him, do. Get all things Victor needs, a place to make the bride.... The Bartletts are nice and will understand Abner's helping his friend. Philippa and the children are nice.... No bride and family for the monster no good families for Bartlett and Holt. Everyone needs their family. The monster does."

He stood up there awhile, saying such things to me, repeating them carefully to make sure I understood. I was so sickened I could scarcely determine his motivation for repetition. It was surmise: Curiously the monster seemed possessed of a weird innocence. He was his own center and, if he had a conscience, it must certainly not be what we would call conscience, not the Tao, not natural law, not an innate moral being, not the spirit of man. Whatever was right for him was right. Simply. If it was not right for him, *it wasn't right.* That was why Clairson was killed, because he was not right for the monster. His righteousness easily wore the face of innocence because he believed in his innocence. He *could not* do wrong. This is what he believed. He felt unbeholden to acknowledge Victor's superiority over him even though Victor had made him. With practice, I thought, *we* could go the same way in disregard of our maker.

After awhile he stopped. In the distance above I heard faint crackings and rustlings. The smell had receded, too. I remained taut and clutching my covers, listening a long time. Then thought rushed in upon me, a flood of tactical and logistic concerns, the most of which concerned my own family, Bartletts and Holts (Philippa's married name), and neighborhood. Then I thought of how I was to help Victor get everything. See the blacksmith about parts for the apparatus (about which I knew almost nothing)? A consultation with Dr. Kimball, perhaps?

Of course I would not be saying one word about the monster or what Victor would be doing with the things he needed. I began to think, too, about just where the monster-creation might take place. At that time there were few houses to let in village or town: houses were built by newcomers or re-created from pieces of other houses when a settler came to town. ...I could not bring myself to think about where the body would—*what* the new monster would be made of. It was horrifying. No, I thought, this cannot be real, cannot be happening.

Philippa and the children are nice. Philippa and the children are nice. The rush of thought carried me onward, pushing me up and out of the crooks. Before I knew what was happening I found myself stumbling about beneath the big trees. I had vocalized nothing but would not have been surprised had I heard myself gibbering or screaming up through the far branches toward the heavens.

I stopped, leaned into a big spruce trunk, holding onto its roughness and scent as I had to my father when a child. Once upon a time he had gone to war with the Sandy River militia and the Continental Army.

I thought: *I'm not going to do one thing the monster tells me.*

The good thing about it was that now, as allowed by the monster, I'd be able to confer with Victor. Just how this was to come about and under what conditions remained to be seen. I looked around, found my stuff and settled back into the crooks, this time sitting cross-legged leaning against a tree. After the promise I'd made to myself I felt calmer. I prayed, wondering if I had the strength to keep this promise, hold fast my resolve. I sat resting against the tree, letting the sounds of the woodland seep into me. Sit still long enough they will come. A soft moth-like fluttering of bats too near for comfort, the chirping of tree frogs, wavering loon call in the dark overhead, rabbits a bit spring-crazed and hunting one another, the owl again. More softly now the rustle of mice or voles beneath the leaf cover. The demonic scream of a bobtail cat higher on Jasper Mountain. The sudden gigantic *whump* a tree, great tree, falling for no evident reason in the distance.

The next thing I knew was Victor's low speaking, as he crouched down beside me. His skunk smell invaded me. I wakened with a start, quiet morning light filling the woods, fresh from the earth's turn toward the sun.

"You heard it all? You are to help me? Abner...."

"I'm awake." He stood and I stared up at him. His face was gaunt and haggard, his beard thicker. I handed him up a blanket and he tied it round at his neck for warmth. Victor's form twitched with impatience. He scratched at his neck between the knotted blanket and beard. He smelled of skunk, his eyes black and penetrating. He was focused to a very fine point. I had seen him exceeding tense but not so keen-edged as now.

"He's going to hurt Regina."

Stiffly I unwound and stood, steadying myself against the tree. "No. I'm going to kill him."

"Please be quiet." He looked about. "—We just don't know...."

He stepped back and started to move away. "Please come."

Swiftly I gathered up my stuffs and came after him, tugging my bedroll together as I walked. He stopped short.

"Is this the way to Gottheim?"

I gestured through the woods. "We go down through here and join the road beyond the settlement. If anyone comes, maybe a wagon or ox-cart, we can get a ride."

He said, "I don't like to be seen—can't see what it might mean for us. I must at least become presentable before I show myself. This —," he self-gestured, "I've become a tramp. That cannot be good for any purpose."

We were stumbling down through the woods, over deadfall, through fallen twigs and years of dead leaves. As we got near the Tuelltown Road thickets increased and we were pushing the brambles out of our faces. The frost had only recently softened out of the rutted road we now walked. For a mile or two we talked it over, Victor more vocal and hardly listening. I was so excited that it was a while before I recognized our discontinuity.

Have you ever talked along with someone in supposed agreement, thinking you know the other's mind, only to stop amazed against a wall of startling obstruction? You can only blame yourself for not seeing it sooner. I had thought that surely there was nothing to do now but go straight to Mother's household and get my father's firearm. As Victor kept on I saw that he had no intention of tackling the problem head on. I thought now he might be for doing exactly as the monster wanted. —It almost seemed like he was not even going to but pretend the manufacture of —.

"Victor!" I almost hollered but caught myself in time, glancing around. "Where is the monster?!"

This brought us both up short. While I had his attention I said, "What about Clairson?!"

"Shortly after I came back to Regina, I got a letter from the Griswolds saying he was rumored missing. He's dead. The monster killed him. Didn't you hear it?" He sounded irritated.

I could not wipe the heightened revelatory disgust out of my face, I gawped at him. "You said it! —He's going to kill Regina. And who knows who else will get hurt?!"

He stopped, looking at me with those penetrating dark eyes. "I didn't thank you for coming after me. I mean it. If you had not found me,... if you had not gripped me."

Aback, I mumbled my welcome. "...If I had not seen the white robin...." It was too disarming, and I felt I *needed* to be armed. Was this an evasion?

"...White robin? What—"

"Victor, it almost seems like you are really going to make this... thing."

"No. Not that, Abner." It was firmly said.

Suddenly his glance shot into the woods above us. Thinking the monster was come, I turned but saw only a very white and wizened old man climbing on his spindles over a stone wall still in the making. I had never seen him before and was completely taken by his appearance. What in the world could such an old man like that mean coming out of the woods, or even being in the woods on this mountain in the first place? He was so decrepit, his shanks so monstrously thin, and his disengagement from all comfort so evident (he should have been sitting by the fire bundled up in a quilt) that a feeling of pity pierced me.

"Oh grandfather," I said, "what are you doing out here all alone?" I climbed over the ditch choked with briar canes to help him cross. His homemade buckskins hung on him as on a scarecrow. They seemed so light-colored as to be almost bleached by the sun, very thin and ragged. At least he had a staff of knotted polished wood, a stick stripped of bark and weathered to the color of bone. It made me wonder if it was as old as he.

I said, "Where are you going? Where do you live?" As yet he had answered me nothing except to give a very feeble giggle, along with a frighteningly silly almost toothless grin when I helped him descend into the road.

The gold of the morning had turned to silver, as mist and cloud drifted in from the west. Here the road was flanked by the woods. All the twigs stretching upward were swollen and red with the slow coming of spring and the descending damp. I took note of this and hoped it would not rain, especially for the sake of this feeble creature before me. The more I looked the more his decrepitude astonished and worried me.

"Please, Uncle," I said, thinking perhaps to quiet my nerves by using the community's euphemism indicating less age than does the word grandfather. "What is your name?"

"*Hee-hee-hee.* Jaspah-snowy-moundon... *hee-hee-hee.* Jaspa-snowy-forehead."

"Isn't that some form of the Indian name for Jasper Mountain?" Victor said. "He's suffering deep dementia."

"Do you live in the settlement yonder?" I gestured eastward back along the road toward the hamlet. He only giggled, mucus a'drip from his nose, his wispy-white head bobbling on his neck which was thrust forward. "You can't live in Gott'im!" I pointed that way, certain it was too far. The road would be curving around the base of the mountain, but anyone of greater quality and strength could have climbed through the woodland and puckerbrush by a shorter if more troublesome way.

He laughed shrilly, the more. "I would not fit! *Hee-hee-hee.*"

"Abner." Victor spoke. "You will either have to take him back to the settlement or carry him along to Gottheim with us. The only other way is to leave him here. We must be on our way. I can go ahead if that's the way it must be, and you can bring him along. We've got—"

"Victor! Don't tell me we've got to be about the monster's business!" —Bit of poetry, that, I thought later— "This old soul is trembling, needs our help, and if we have to stop and comfort him, feed and warm him, we will do so. I can't leave him alone anymore than I could have left you alone!"

Victor stood cloaked in the lousy old blanket, a frown lowering his brow. Sharply he said, "This is what we were going to be saved from! This creature is what we are coming to, what everyone is coming to— at best! This hideous permutation. Can't you see what a travesty this is for any maker? You keep forbearing to acknowledge it! —Can't you see there must be no potent, no present—"

Instead of wisely ignoring the non sequitur about God running away from us, I said, "*This* hideous mutation! What is that monster, some delicate primrose fresh from his creator's hand? If this sick old man is our future, we still must care for it—care for *him.* Our duty is to him in this moment right now and that monster be damned!"

"— That monster is going to kill Regina. He's going to wreak havoc in Gott'im."

I thought about this a moment, deeply suspicious. I could not deny the truth of it, but the motivation behind his speaking...? I said, quietly,

"I think not," gathering all the dignity into it that I could muster. "He may not need me, but he needs *you*. Why, he needs Regina as much or more than he needs me. He knows he will not get one thing out of you if he hurts her."

"What of your family, of the Village? You cannot say the same of them.... —You will not be able to lead him.... Look." He pointed and I turned to see the old man floundering up out of the ditch with his stick. He was already trying to clamber back over the stone wall, like some spindly-jointed spider ready to cast off its outworn carapace.

Over my shoulder I said, "I will meet you in Gott'im. *You* least have wit enough to get there and appear to have the strength!" I hurried through the ditch following grandfather and, without looking back, climbed over the wall and went into the woods after him.

But I heard Victor call after me, "Do not think of me what you are thinking! And watch out, he will try to kill you. Both you and the old man!" Already the damp was thickly descending, muffling his words with distance. "...I have my duty too...."

Vexed and torn, I followed after the little old white man, still faintly gleaming through the boles.

How can he get on so fast? I wondered, picking my way through the underbrush.

I quickened my pace, fighting through the stems, calling. I could no longer see him. Suddenly I heard him behind me, *Hee-hee-hee*. I turned, startled out of my wits. He sat in the crooks leaning against a tree, his bony knees splayed, legs jutting, his white staff lying near.

His voice pitched high, he said, "Fetch your firearm! Fetch your hatchet! I'll slay the monstah fah ye! *Hee-hee-hee, hee-hee-hee.*"

His pale buckskin rags near falling off him, he was shivering with cold and giggling like he hadn't a care in the world.

I let drop my stuff, reached into my bosom to feel for the fire kit I kept in a pouch on a thong around my neck. Then I started to gather up twigs blown down in the winter gales.

Who could have let such a thing happen? How could someone in any of these settlements let one of their old wander off this way? It is unchristian, it is dereliction, it's stupidity, it's... it should be criminal!

It was almost unheard of for one to reach such a great age: most people died far younger than this of injury or disease. I couldn't help thinking how much more merciful when God did as promised: It is surely said in the Scripture but three score and ten for length of life. Oh, this is unjust, but what can I do: I cannot kill the man myself, Lord!

I was mumbling all this as I started to work over the shavings and dried evergreen with knife and flint. Everything was becoming damp. I happened to look up then and noticed my charge had gone again. By now I was truly cursing under my breath. "Forgive me, Lord, but this man should have died!" I stood, got very quiet, and glanced all around the dripping misted woods.

There a little way above me to the westward moved a thickening of the mist, — had to be him, had to. I should have fed him from my dried meat and warmed him, but I'd been too distrait to think of opening my bedroll to throw the covers on him. Still trying to keep my eyes on the movement above, I gathered my things together again and started off after him through the boles. *Now how could <u>you</u> let this happen? Here you are blaming all in and out of creation and now you are doing it yourself!*

How can he have so much energy, how can he be shivering with cold and going ahead of me, on and on? I began to surprise myself with curious thoughts: If I had not had that conversation with Victor, Victor's seeing this man, commenting on him, been torn asunder from what we were doing.... This cannot *possibly be* a woods-queer delusion...? I might even start thinking that Victor and the monster were delusions, that there really was such a thing as a crazed poetic temperament, that people *will* go crazy living in the woods alone.

But no. There he was, under that damp-blackened great white pine. I felt such relief at seeing him... but it was combined with an awful letdown: Now I would truly have to take care of this crumbling old wreck and see to it that he lived through the night. I climbed up toward him and off he went again. I cannot say how often this happened, but the woods began to darken and the mystery of his going on defeated me: Always he kept just in sight, always I scrambled to approach, always he eluded me through the mist. *How can this be?*

I even had time to think of other things, so used did I get to his leading me on, hour after hour, now into the dark. Things such as, where is the monster — must have followed after Victor. That's fine! — hope I never see either one of them again. There's no way they can make a monster and hinder the knowledge of *that* round Gott'im! Folly. Laughable. Someone is going to see and shoot that thing, sure. You can't just walk into Melville's and order up a body to come in a wagon. Why not order individual parts through mail-order and fashion your bride from the latest monster materials? Get the miller to grind you out one! Have the choir sing it into existence! Maybe that new poet Lord Byron could incantate one for you. I was fairly entertaining myself now. Another moment and I'd be rolling around the woods in laughter, gathering up leaves and breaking up sticks, hitting my head on the rocks. *Where was the terror of the monster?* Then, in my pursuit, I began to notice the ground dipping downward.

Mother's House

It had not rained. The mist cleared out of the sky as dusk fell, and now through the stems of the trees I saw them: lights: like the soft glow of fireflies scattered throughout the trees, being the dearest sight I could remember seeing in a long time. It was the village of Gottheim spread out in evening light, the lights of the dear small houses, set before the greater reflecting light of Ben Hutchins's Pond, some of it still in ice. There was even a light burning in his grist mill.

I went straight down through the trees to pond's edge and took the path back up through the woods, all the way round to the other side where stood a straggling settlement. Our log house stood off from it behind the field. This field had been handpicked of rocks, its edges hemmed with the stones themselves heaped into orderly walls. It waited to dry out for the plowing, to come once the danger of frost was passed. My siblings and I had helped to pick out all those rocks, and, in fact, I was still at the picking every season after the frost.

The latch was out and I went right in, straight to the redly glowing hearth and took down father's long-barreled flintlock musket. I set it on the table and took the kit off the mantelpiece to clean it; removed the ramrod, picked up the wedge drift and tapped the wedge out of the plates. I half-cocked and lifted the barrel out of the stock. I heard the stair creak and mother come down; holding a candle in her hand, through the front parlor she came.

"Why, Abner, it's good to see you. What ah you doing with that?" Her voice was a bit sharp following her initial much softer greeting.

That's what I like about mother. Straight to the point after expressing due gratitude. She's a gangling, odd looking woman, this night dressed in a night shirt, but some days actually outfitted in father's old gear. From the outland, they sometimes called her, even to her face, for she's not ill-humored. Her no-frills mobcap was askew and salt-and-pepper hair a'straggle. She cared too little for her looks to suit a young son's vanity, but father never cared I guess.

I thought of the old man who had lead me a goose chase, me winding up in Gottheim, anyhow, without him. I said, "I don't think you'd understand." I thought of the monster. "You wouldn't understand."

"You betta rest and eat. You ah wrought ovah." She stopped, seeing I kept at it, then added, with a bit of asperity, "You might work a li'l betta you take off that bedroll and those pouches."

I kept working. She set the candle on the table, shedding a pool of light on my hands a-fumble, cleaning the breech end of the barrel. I think she went to the hearth and built up the fire, then went down the cellar steps where she kept the churn, came back up with some buttermilk, set it on the table, and ladled out some stew. I did not realize this until I sat back in my chair, exhausted, and looked out on the meager but wholesome meal, that stew from the bottom of the barrel, saltmeat left over from last year. I was famished.

She said, "You wouldn't had to do that you cleaned it good last time, young man. You know that thing'll rust you don't."

I could barely move to the other side of the table, and her chair, where I then plunked myself down. I allowed her to lift off the bedroll, but thought better of losing the pouches and nudged her away. I fed myself ravenously, mechanically, my mind busy over the better path for getting to Besiegt's, as best I could recollect where it lay.

My mouth was full. "You know any little old quee-ah drastic greezy man runs around in bleached buckskin, tattered, white hair down to his shoulders, bald pate on top? Moves a bit faster'n he ought fah being so old. I don't remember him."

She had gone over to my chair and was probing to the breech-plug with the rod, just a dite too forcefully. I guessed she was thinking, *How you talk!*, and, *You expect me to do all your chores for you*. I had left a lot undone to go out in the woods and feel sorry for myself. There was still a good half-ton of rocks in that field out there, pushed up this winter past.

Now she worked thoughtfully, back-and-forth in the barrel with short strokes. At last she said, "Can't think of a one would dress like that. Few evah get like that round here.... Lest they go in the woods too long...."

Was this supposed to be a hint? Naturally she was waiting for me to say why. I didn't. I was, after all, alive these eighteen winters and not some suckling who tells all his business. If I'd been alive thirty winters I'd have said without thought as a matter of courtesy, but I was too young to know that, yet. That is, I would have described the old man and told how I found him and something of how he had got away. Not if I lived to be a hundred would I have said anything about the monster. At 100 I would have been too demented to, anyway. I was having a hard time believing in the monster myself, off and on, but you could not have told that for my actions.

No no, I thought. *He's real, he's real. We are in deep trouble....Victor, yes. Victor's real....* The hackles were rising again. I said cautiously, "You know the Besiegts? Ovah town? Older son by the name of Victor?"

"Gott'im schoolmaster while back? They said he was here of late. Now gone up to Boston or one of them places to get ready for his intended, that young lady lives with them."

I could hear her asking why I asked. She didn't, however. I had been planning to jump right up and finish the job on that firearm, but the next thing I knew was pain and stiffness in my neck. I opened my eyes and saw sunlight from the shutter in thin outline on the wall opposite. My head was on the table, which was clean as a whistle. I felt for my pouches—still in place—and sat up. Turning my head, I saw the flintlock disappeared from over the mantel in morning light.

I jumped up, ready to accuse, ready to holler up the stairs, but my gaze snagged on the firearm, dressed and ready, leaning next the door frame. As usual I didn't waste more than a half moment feeling ashamed. Even without that kind readiness, it would've been folly to think of mother still lying abed. I tipped the ladle into the stew for a sup, then pocketed powder and shot from the mantelpiece and slung the heavy flintlock on my back below the bedroll.

Oh but that sun was bright, strong spring sun. After a trip to the privy, I stood there gazing across the forest-edged, neglected, stubbled field a moment. *But the monster...*

I started down the path toward the lane, then looked over my shoulder to see the cellar doors open and mother sitting there in the streaming light, milking Beatrice. I walked down to say goodbye. The cellar I saw, with both relief and shame, was mucked out.

As I approached, she said, "Late getting to this. I had to get Buster back into the sty, to be bred. Old man Howe is driving his boar ovah today."

I looked over at the pigpen, downwind of the house, where the ambiguously named Buster lay sleeping and snoring, looking a bit like a small bleached-out mud hill. The thought fleeted through my mind that I could sorely use a bath.

"I... I thank you, mother." I fingered the butt-end of the flintlock behind me, hoping she would see and take my meaning.

A stream of milk hit the side of the bucket, but I was only watching for Mother's face.

"That's all right." She kept at it, watching the streams, head resting a bit against Beatrice's side. She had on father's dark old home spun hunting frock, still holding together after hard use in the old war.

I turned to start back, but stopped. "How old was he— how did Victor Besiegt's mother die?"

Remember, reader, death, the care of those approaching death, the handling of the dead, all fell on us in our houses, the preponderance of those dead being children. Two of my brothers died before we could know them. My father was gone before he was much more than a set of knees to me. We did not get used to its sorrow but it was common, untimely, and intimate to us, known: we dealt with it so.

She looked up then. "The lockjaw. Why I remember it."

I turned back and, coming out from the cellar way, walked on toward the lane. Here was something to think of, and I did all the way to the village.

It is difficult to picture the horror of this disease, its germs alive in the soil, and especially in the muck of the road, and well able to flourish in deeply wounded human tissue without benefit of oxygen. For a child to witness his mother healthy one day, injured the next and with this dread disease besetting within maybe a week or two.... All the muscles are tautly pulled, the bodily frame bent rigid like a bow. It is as though rigor mortis sets in with its death's head before the body, and the light of the eyes, has mercifully died. Nature flings off the beauteous face of the beloved. Nature's own beauteous face is flung aside like a curtain to reveal the awfulness of our condition in true degrading horror and awe. Christian brethren, you marvel at what you may deem the insipid deism of our age, our intellectuals embracing (if that is the right word) of the absent God. But think, when you are watching your helpful, harmless loved one grow more rigid by the hour, wearing the grin of death, at last after numerous days to die in the torture of convulsion: Would not you, may be, find more sense or even comfort in the idea of a far off impersonal God? One who was not so present as to be aware of your loved one's agony and do nothing to hinder it: For is not God God? Is God helpless? (Yes, there may be a few holes to be poked in this idea and send it flying in tatters... but not now.)

Is it a wonder, that the *Person* who hung on the cross in an agony said, "*Father* forgive them for they know not what they do?"

It is a wonder. *There* surely was one who believed in a personal God.

And as I approached the cabins and white houses of New England Gottheim gathered round their green common before the great pond still scummed in patches of rotten ice... I believed that Victor was forgiven his misguided science and its application... though I understood that we would still have to live with its consequences.

Thoughts of the sufferings which occur, ever so untimely, in these houses, were heightened by the contrast I felt between the sufferers and the placid fronts as I made my way beyond the Common down School Street past houses, church and village school. I would be watched from any window, wherever someone sat nigh a loved one injured or ill, as surely as I was by those who greeted me, one or two by name, looking across the yard from their work; mostly women at the spring cleaning, boiling the laundry, or at the slaughtering. I looked longest at the white Georgian massive splendor of Dr. Kimball's house with its many divided lights reflecting the blue of sky above. Should any attempt be made to stop in there? I began dramatizing my meeting with the great doctor, one of two or three great intellects (and also a literary man) in the Town. I shook my sad, self-mocking head and kept going, the heavy buckskin-dressed flintlock on my back growing heavier and heavier.

Thanks to the Yankee rebellion, a colony no longer, but now of the District of Maine of the Commonwealth of Massachusetts, the village was roughhewn in this far and hidden outpost beneath Jasper Mountain. Our remoteness told daily in the amount of hard work it was to keep life going in the form which it had, the form given to us. Simply, we had to keep going, no matter what, until we were no longer able. This is not the same motion as boldly seizing the moment in a fit of "inspiration," such as I had attempted with my poetry and the Boston publishing house.

And all this brought me back, as I headed into the wilderness again, to thoughts of the suffering and endurance of being. I felt, with Victor, the difficulty of being which he had put me onto. (For another instance, why should those silly thoughts about seeking out the great doctor keep recurring to me after they are rejected?... and this was a very slight instance of a lack of control over my being. These false notes of the soul—one would expect to be more in charge of his soul than he is able to be over the illnesses of his body.)

The road to the Besiegt's was the same as the Twombly Town Road; and the land opened up beneath the spreading mountains for the river valley, as I left the small turnings of Gottheim. The fearsome echo of the monster's screaming and howling, his chuffing and hissing laughter, came back to me almost audibly and I shuddered. Then I remembered his words, snatches of his conversation, and it seemed to me that his awful noises may even be some brute indication of a suffering I might recognize. Animal expressions of a sentient being... in pain.

You will think I was softening toward him. May be. How could he help but be lonely — being, anywhere in all creation, the sole of his kind? How could he help but feel betrayed by the Griswolds, who had called him, in their several ways, friendly helper? An unbranded murderer, hunted everywhere, surely despised, feared, and not pitied by his maker. And now he thought he saw a way to gain companionship, sympathy, a life— not among men, as I had heard Victor caution him—but someplace in the wild: an outcast, but with his feminine counterpart. He too wanted to cast out his own suffering and gain absolute control over his being... which, he believed, also meant controlling absolutely all around him. It was a vain dream, and I knew it. No matter the boldness involved, it would never work. Something else *would* come of it— more consequences—but not what you dream. Again I said to myself, I am not going to do one thing the monster says.

I walked the verges of the soft fields, this road being muddy and rutted. There came up the smell of horse muck as I by-passed a clump. That whiff made me remember again the agony of Victor's mother's death. The unmelodious singing of robins and calling of the ravens could scarcely banish it. There was their house now, tiny at the end of a long lane and I cut across lots toward it. There were no leaves to hamper the view while I tried to penetrate the woods beyond it with my gaze.

I saw nothing out of the usual and no movement among the numerous stems, the woodland carrying down through to the river.

I looked back toward the house again, a solid timber frame dwelling, with carriage house and barn behind. The lines of the structures were clean and Roman, based on the splendid neoclassical architecture, elegant and popular, of 18th-century New England and splendorous slave-built Jeffersonian Virginia. These two dwellings, of Dr. Kimball and Dr. Besiegt, were the primary anomalies that contrasted so sharply with the rest of the more rustic town. Even the miller's house was not so pleasant.

The Conjoined Twins

I did not knock upon the front but went round to the back door, sure of my station, for all the republicanism breathed into us by the Revolution, and the sturdy no-nonsense self-respecting Yankee Puritan demeanor impressed on us from our birth. Social equality, what was that? We were equal before the law, in political responsibility and opportunity to rise, I guessed, but society was not governed by it. I was somewhat dismayed to find Regina herself open the door; and, beneath the lacy mobcap covering her pretty auburn hairdo, she gazed at me a question out of gentle troubled features. I felt keenly my dishevelment.

I saw myself instantly through her eyes, a grubby, pockmarked youth, with grizzled jawline, the scraggling wispy beard of my non-shaving sojourn in the woods. I was lousy though she probably didn't notice. I don't think I smelled too good, either. The only good part of it was that I had not dramatized this meeting beforehand and so had no reason to be more embarrassed than I felt at that moment.

But then it was as though she looked past me, asking, "Are you here for the meal?"

"—Good day, Miss Regina, may I speak with Victor—the younger Dr. Besiegt, please?"

She seemed doubtful. Her voice was soft. "... I'm afraid I can't help you." She smiled faintly with distracted regret and began closing the door.

I stood there a moment, bemused myself, wondering what to do next. I turned and glanced off across the weedy sparsely greening field toward Gottheim and the darkling flank of Jasper Mountain, a few patches up there also vaguely greening. The door opened wide before it had closed, and Regina peered out, saying, "Are you Abner Bartlett?"

"Yes!" My response was too instant and emphatic, jarring her. But her uncertainty seemed to vanish and she welcomed me in with quiet warmth.

I removed the firearm and set it down inside the door. She led me, past garden implements and coats hanging in the shed I hardly noticed, into the kitchen, where the woman and a girl were working at the sideboard and iron sink. With the simmering fragrance from the hearth it was plain that preparations for the noon meal were ongoing.

"I do remember you, Abner. Please sit down." Regina gestured, and I sat thoughtless on a bench beneath the window to watch the cooking as she left the room for what she said would be but a few moments.

I looked over my shoulder out the window into the young reddening orchard — too young for bearing —and saw the old man pruning, shearing or pinching a bit, then standing back to see the effect. The woman stood at the hearth, stirring, and she spoke to me. I started, then turned back.

"How's mother, Abner?"

I gave her my attention and saw that it was Mrs. Crockett from Twombly. She used to live on our side of the pond when she was a Rowe, a bit younger than mother. I remembered vaguely that they kept bees over there upon the hillside in the woods. Her brother once said he got good with the flintlock on delectating bears on account of those bees. They also milked the trees for sap and so had a good sweet household, Mother always said.

I did not say Mother was worried for her son; I said, "Good, Miz Crockett. Saw her this morning...."

It was rude, but I was distracted and wanted to think: I turned back toward the window. She seemed to accept this without resentment, saying something to the girl. Hearing but snatches, I let their talk pass over me, the sweet ordinariness of life I had forgone these weeks in the wild. *Victor must be here... but the monster?...*

On Regina's return into the kitchen, her pale gown and apron faintly rustling near me, I turned and looked up, the idea leaping into my mind: Is she to be his next victim? The thoughts flashed in my mind of Clairson disappeared, of the torn squirrels and the white skunk. My imagination was heightened, and I thought she might smell the skunk on me even at that moment.

Amid the clinking of pewter or tinware against the crockery, places were being set on the table, and at that moment I heard as though the tromping of a troop in through the shed, and looked to see the few workers about the place, and maybe two or three paupers coming in for the meal. They had seemed to appear of nowhere, for I had seen no one but Uncle Jordan, who had been at the pruning. Regina said, "Would you like to stay for the meal, Abner?... after your errand."

I but nodded and followed her out of the room, looking back once to see them all seated and bowing their heads, the low ruminative sound of prayer coming out to me as I passed through, peering into the dining room. There I glimpsed a locally famous painting of Prometheus in oils by the celebrated colonial painter, John Singleton Copley (as he was when he painted this copy of the mythic figure). Below was a welcoming scented fire on the hearth. In a haze of distraction, I noticed three glimmering places set at the gleaming table, I guessed for the family: Regina, Greenleaf, and old Dr. Besiegt... all but Victor, maybe...? I was thinking again of Regina, and how she was to be the bride... and those in the kitchen, I thought now, her guests; the guests of her bounty and patronage. Then I remembered there were those among them who had earned it, and the shocking stray thought occurred to me: she is in their debt as well. Was she even in debt to the others, the paupers, for giving her a chance to serve?

I remember the steep narrow stair winding to the upper rooms, and Victor sitting behind the gently opening door in one, clothed in what I took to be a dressing gown. I had never seen one before. There was a fire softly snapping and a great four-poster. I wondered if there were other such great furnishings in all the sleeping chambers. I caught sight of a copper bath behind a screen, and thought vaguely of who would have put it there, brought up the hot water: Was the household aware of his presence? But immediately my attention went back to Victor. Regina was gone, and the door closed.

He was freshly shaved, his dark hair clean and fluffed out, his dark eyes piercing, as ever, looking at me. "I'm glad to see you made it, and so quickly."

He did not ask me about the old man or what I had been doing.

With a touch of pique, I said, "I brought the musket." I stood looking at him until he gestured for me to sit on the bed, neatly made. The genuine glazed windows were still steamed from his bath and, beyond, the white of daylight was in one, the dark of the mountain in the other.

He ignored about the flintlock, glanced down at the broadside he was holding and said, "Perhaps Mr. Moore should rethink his attack on Mr. Jefferson. Parts of it are fine: I agree with what he says about slavery; however, he fails to consider well the remnants of abandoned sea life on the mountain tops. Such upheaval will take far longer than 6000 years to accommodate." He lay the broadsheet on the bed, saying carelessly, "Take that with you if you like."

I glanced at it, folded and stuck it in my blouse. Reading material is hard to come by, and always welcome.

"I just got here a little while ago, myself." He looked away a moment, his gaze playing along the top of the scrollwork on a great wardrobe. He looked back "Thank you, Abner, for coming, for seeing me through as far as you have done."

Was it perfunctory, the thing to say? A morsel to keep me going? "I guess I'm not done, yet."

Victor was silent. He gazed at me. I began to feel a bit uncertain but sat working at maintaining my composure. It was all new, being in this household, sitting here in a bedchamber talking like this with the eminent scientist and metaphysician. Fresh from the bath, he seemed newly minted.

"The workers must have thought I was a tramp, coming here like I did. I made her send me away but then contrived to come in at the cellar. I wanted to remain down there, but she insisted on this, 'At least', she said. She has matured. Beyond me, I think. ...Greenleaf has been helping her with me. Abner, they have no idea. She is mystified but asks me no question.... Thank God. We must keep it that way."

"But what does she think you've been doing?... or can't you guess what she thinks? How did you begin chasing the monster, even... or is that *vice versa*?"

"Very astute of you," he said dryly. "We met, that's all. Yes, he surprised me by being here in Gottheim, by knowing my household. He intercepted me on my way back to Cambridge to prepare for her coming. I did think I was chasing him after he made certain threats. He's quite uncanny... or perhaps I should say canny?"

Heating up I said, "The proud father, you? He cannot have done this without everyone knowing, surely?"

"You know Gott'im." It was sharply put. "Nothing's known but what it's talked of. No, there's no word of him anywhere. The word *is* canny. Apparently he's learned some tricks since his sojourn on the Massachusetts Bay, our city upon a hill. I'm not going into it."

I was distracted a moment by the reference to our ancestors, then trying to remember where Besiegt, as a name, had come from and what was his mother's maiden name so as to place him among the Puritan descent. But I plunged heedless ahead as he said,

"Will you help me, Abner?"

"Yes. I'm set now: I can do the job. Where is he?"

He was thoughtful. "We must have a plan. This may very well involve getting started on his proposal.—"

"—You are out of your mind. We need to kill him and be done with it. Where is he?"

"Abner, it is not so easy. I have a whole household here to worry about, let alone—. There is Greenleaf and my father—. At the very least we must distract him, give him a show."

"I'd say he's canny," I muttered trying to throw as much sarcasm into it as possible. "I thought you told me not to think of you as helping him? How can I do that with you being so indirect. Don't you want to go straight at it? This is not God's being! He is some awful great creation of Victor Besiegt!... Maybe that's why you now can't bring yourself to —"

"I suppose Abner Bartlett is going to tell me about being, what it takes to *make be*? What it *means*? *Who* is responsible for it?"

"Who's *monstah* that?" I almost shouted but remembered in time to keep my voice down. I was so indignant I could not keep seated, and stood up to pace a bit before the window. I rubbed a spot and looked out to see Uncle Jordan still at the pruning. There was the older blossoming orchard beyond him, trees tall enough to ride beneath, and he had set a blaze — brightly flaming — of discarded branches. Vaguely I thought that wasteful, as apple wood makes such good kindling. I could not remember whether or not he had come in to dinner. Then I forgot about Regina's meal and turned back to face Victor waiting for me to come out of my pique. I said, "Yes, the monster thinks, therefore he is." I chuckled helplessly. "... I wish I knew what *you* were thinking...." I could say nothing more then but to recite: " 'O ye sons of Men, how long will you turn my glory into shame? Surely God will not hear vanity, neither will the Almighty regard it.' "

Quietly he said, "We do not know where we are at here, Abner. You are spouting."

When I heard that— I was going to preach over him with my pride. But something checked me.

Then the image of mother milking Beatrice after chasing down Buster came to me. I stopped. I thought, If I'd been doing what I was supposed to... none of this would have happened—to me, anyway....

And maybe I would have been able to take care of the monster on my own home ground, had it been necessary.

"Yes," I said softly. "Maybe. I'll grant it, the spouting." I went and sat down again, saying low, "*But I'm not going to do anything the monster....*" I didn't care whether Victor heard me but hoped it would not bring the great thing out of the wardrobe on me.

"Where is he, Victor? Did you see him on your way here?"

"I don't know. He *is*, that's all. And very near. Abner, I gave him my word I would get started on this, and for the sake of everyone here and in Gottheim... and for other reasons, among them trying to figure this whole thing out, I must begin. This will mean going to Bangor. But you must stay behind and guard them. Will you do it?"

"Of course I will guard them!"

I sensed instant relief on his part, and, given his usual self possession, was surprised to recognize just how concentrated, and perhaps distressed, he had been until this moment.

I pressed on. "I will guard all of Gott'im!"

"... I don't think—. You will think I am being selfish. Abner, it is that I do not think one man can do all that. And I believe it is my own he is after. He is—exceedingly jealous."

I was silent, thinking. I said, "Dr. Besiegt, it is hard not to be vexed... I guess you'll grant it.... You gave your *word* to the monster? Do you mean your word under extortion is your bond to the brutish? Do you mean the monstrous is *trusting* you to keep your word? *believes* in your word? What does your word mean anymore? I mean I could think of one hundred ludicrous explanations for *all* of this. You made a monster, you ran off from the monster without teaching him anything, he probably killed your best friend, possibly tore apart a household in Cambridge, is threatening *all* your loved ones, and the entire community of Gottheim..." my voice sank: "and you gave and intend to keep your word."

He was silent. Then, "Mr. Bartlett, you have a way... like no other... of making me feel ashamed."

Again he was silent. Then he sighed. "Perhaps it is just, since it is you accusing me."

Mr. Bartlett is the only one who knows of it, hence he is the only one with such power. I sighed in my turn. I was not going to get an answer. I could only mutter, and be content with the sop to my pride.

He continued. "... I think I owe you an apology. I happen to agree with what you said, your quotation of scripture. Granting that God is glorious however impersonal and remote, granting that it is a shame to meddle with powerful principles and applications for which we cannot know the consequences —. Perhaps if we knew the principles enough to know the consequences and so avoid them.... But we do not. I did not. There are too many details, all with their own consequences. All the same, I wonder. Will the Almighty, and by that I mean, the physical laws, regard our vanity? The laws will redound, is this disregarding?..." He was thoughtful.

It occurred to me that he was thinking of that peculiar moment, in which he did not obey the slight urge to stay his hand, and the entrance of that fatal helping hand of lightning which was additional to his inadequate voltaic pile. Because in that one moment Victor found the stricture too gentle, even accommodating, it brought the monster to life. Was it accommodating? The laws in place accommodating to the action of free will? With my faith in a personal God I could but wonder, and it was not out of the question that Victor should. I thought now he would have wanted the rod of iron to step in and forbid him. To break him in pieces, if necessary. Both him and his monster.

"I often think of the book of Job, Abner. Not that I am worthy of being any Job, any *such*. I am too selfish in my pursuits. But if you consider the question of free will. In the story, it is only that wager, that game between the God and Satan, limning, or even making possible, freedom of will." He looked away. "Oh those inimitable ancestors of ours, those Puritans. It is hard to throw them off, keep their ghosts from tempting us. But think, Abner," he looked back at me, "they are not only Job's friends, but they bequeath us Job's friends to our very souls.... I sometimes think our souls are made up of nothing but Job's friends."

I had never thought of it like that before. I wanted to think on it a moment, but found myself resisting all thought but one. One great troublous thought: I had just given Victor my word to do something *the monster* told me to do. Victor was going to Bangor to make another monster, and I was staying behind as... as an aid in that misbegotten pursuit. My accusation had redounded on me as I remembered the morality of keeping one's word.

Sunlight was beginning to slant into the room through the lights behind Victor. The fire on the grate was dying down, I stood to replenish it with a few sticks by the hearth. This was done without mind, my thought being elsewhere, very worried. Victor was headed in the wrong direction. He should be standing guard his loved ones. I would have to insist on it. He kept on speaking as I listened with but divided attention.

"As the elect, they taught us the harsh personal God with his incongruous personal sacrifice... which could only be based in love, hence incongruous, to their heavy-handedness. Beside that, Abner, why was it necessary since we all suffer the consequence of our nature even so? You will say it's a question of faith in the afterlife. That we would suffer yet more. But think of the narrative like this: Why make so poorly in the first place, if you're going to take a rod to it, rule it with a rod? Why not just put the iron into it in the first place. Wouldn't that make their game— God and Satan—moot? Not to mention less cruel? Make it the way you want it the first time, and then you will not wreck your good name with such cruelties."

There Victor had done it again, managed to throw me into consternation with his intellectualisms. Repaying, I suppose, for the shame I'd heaped on him.

"Yes," he continued, "I've considered well our good ancestors, their goodness as well is their badness. The good in the changing mode of consort, of marriage, through law and custom, was perhaps the best ever known. Equality was most promoted, a true complementary union of woman and man."

You will maybe chuckle? But in the Western tradition it was so in comparison to what went before. And here I break aside to remind the reader of his or her bigotry in assuming the backwardness of all our ancestors. For at base, don't we come, everyone, from a primitive people? We tend to judge, do we not, by our own rules—condemning outright what was the previous good? Rest assured they were essentially even as we are in human nature. Only our superstitions differ, from age to age.

Still speaking of the conceptually evolving Puritan Eve, Victor went behind the screen to dress. I plucked the broadside from my bosom, inspecting it for lice. I unfolded and scanned it, taking note of a curious frontispiece, in miniature, depicting the New England edition of *Aristotle's Masterpiece*. It was a grotesque illustration of Siamese twins. I had heard of them, of course, but to see them in depiction, a true monster of nature, was awe-inspiring. I thought, with a shiver of horror, of Victor's complaint of the story (as he would have it) of the Maker's ill-making. I glanced at the quotation: "Nature to us sometimes does Monsters show,/ That we by them may our own mercies know;/ And there by sin's deformity may see/ In which there's nothing can more monstrous be."

"Temptress or saint," said the voice from behind the screen, "— it was impossible either way. A truer way is more like your Holy Spirit, a comforter."

I could not take my eyes off the deformed creature— two creatures, humans— joined at the side, with but a single pair of legs between them—monstrous yes! I sensed the suffering in the brothers... but did not disagree with the sentiment used at their expense.

"Beauty as a positive good instead of enticement... as, for instance, Milton's Eve. 'Here, in close recess,/ With flowers, garlands, and sweet-smelling herbs,/ Espoused Eve decked first her nuptial bed;/ And heavenly quires the hymenaean sung....'"

Myself yet staring at the two pathetic humans, I quoth, " 'Thus, at their shady lodge arrived, both stood,/ Both turned, and under open sky adored/ The God that made both sky, air, earth, and heaven....'"

"Very good, Abner," came his briefly muffled voice. It was the schoolmaster in him.

He talked on about things alluding to his future bride and his hopes concerning her, never mentioning her in fact. It was reserve and delicacy, in the true Bostonian form. Perhaps it was the restorative normalcy of the setting, his presence among his family, and the nearness of Regina, all combining to help him forget in some measure the sinister presence lurking somewhere without. In a few moments he stepped out from behind the screen, freshly dressed in doveskin breeches, waistcoat and linen blouse, going straight to the glass to brush his dark hair. He had shaved in the bath, and now the dimple in his chin was visible.

He used both brushes. I watched a moment, then said, "You know what I've been thinking, Victor?" He paused then brushed some more, waiting for me to continue. "God cast Adam into a sleep and took material from his side to make his Eve, a suitable help: his love. But when his son was on the cross, they thrust a spear into his side and out came water and blood, in token of what he was doing for his bride. He was not making a monster, but healing a monstrous error— out of his own being. Uniting himself in the whole groaning of the creation which we feel till now."

I saw his image in the mirror stop, a brush still in his hand at his hair. He stood looking at me, reflected in the standing oval glass.

I said, "If only you could thrust your hand into that side, Victor."

Again there was a pause. He said, "Surely you are a poet."

"It just came to me, they sometimes do. Are they true? Is it true, Victor?"

He went on brushing. There was silence, then he said, "True poetry, yes... but may it be true in the way you mean, Abner? ...I think it will be long before we find out if so."

He turned and went to the door, donning his frockcoat. He said, "Use the hot water in the pitchers on the hearth, and the basin there, if you like, the brushes." He gestured toward the dresser. "There is no hurry. I will be in the library until you come down for Regina's dinner. You will not be ill at ease, as I have already told them to expect you from the wilderness in aid of my experimentations.... My father will like you, Abner."

Monster in the Icehouse

When he was gone I jumped up and inspected the blanket I'd been sitting on for white specks. Clean. I went to the hearth, picked up a pitcher and took it to the basin, washed my face and hands and then threw the water into the bath. I went to the glass and tried to smooth down my hair with my fingers. I sighed, loath to mention to my hosts the lousy blanket Victor came here in.

Back downstairs I crept along the passage past a few doors ajar and into the kitchen without, thank goodness, seeing anyone. Remnants of the meal on the table were being cleared, and other food was now carried into the passage (headed for the dining room), by the girl.

"Miz Crockett, can I have some of that bread and butter, please?"

She was busy, her cheeks flushed and wisps of hair straying from her mobcap. "Help yourself fom the table. Help yourself to anathing." She turned away.

"Please see that old blanket gets burned!" I grabbed up something and went quickly through to the shed. She called after, wanting to know my meaning, but I kept going and picked up the musket, then slipped outside, sure Regina would get the message. I went across lots and into the trees, down by the riverside. I wanted to eat sitting on a rock looking out at the flowing water, and think what to do. Then I felt in my pouch for my diary, took out the quill, studied its nib, got out the little phial of ink, and started to write both my thoughts, and a bit of the conversation that had taken place in the upper room. I did not bother my head about what Victor would think of my not showing up for dinner.

What was I to do?

The river below me was flowing, afternoon lights glinting here and there where fine rapids broke the surface. At my back the trees bristled and, beyond, the household would be at work, and Victor preparing to go a journey to Bangor. My standing guard here enabled him to go off after bride-making parts and equipment. I had given my word, now what? I began to pray.

I wrote down a few words of my prayer, packed everything up and followed along the river bank upstream behind the beautifully endowed, efficient Besiegt farmhold. I could but almost see it spread through the trees, except here and there in a flash of white. I rounded a forested bend with the river. There in woods a little above, stood the small windowless ice house made of logs with moss chinking, packed, I suspected, with the winter's harvest of ice. I was a little uneasy, seeing it, becoming contemplative. I thought about ice houses and how useful they might be in helping with certain unorthodox experiments. The cold breeze channeling through the river vale ruffled my hair. I'd taken my hat off before going into the Besiegt house and it was stowed in one of my pouches. On my way to see about that ice house, I dug for it and put it on my head. Then I snatched it off again. I scratched my head all over and examined my fingernails, then went back down to the river and washed my hands and under my fingernails with sand out of a shoreline bar. I don't know why I am so concerned about the Besiegt household, I thought. They must get vermin in there, what with serving the paupers and all.

I don't know why the ice house interested me so—maybe as a workshop for Victor's nefarious purpose?—but there I was, headed toward it in a sort of vacancy of purpose, just waiting, I suppose, for the idea of God to light on me with its guidance. Surely guarding the household means kill the monster if I get the chance. The icehouse was up far enough from the river to avoid any flooding. I opened the creaking door, and there sat the big monster of Victor Besiegt's on the great piled blocks of ice, as though in the lap of luxury. Dwarfing the ice house.

They were stacked to the low rafters behind him. Seated on a lower shelf of ice blocks, he lounged against them. Yes, there was sawdust for insulation, but not enough to make humanly comfortable by any means. His long yellow hair streamed over his shoulders. Scar tissue, holding him together and not hidden by his too small clothes, was clearly visible in light from the open door. Otherwise it had been dark because ice houses are tightly sealed. His gaze had passed over me as I opened the door, I suppose because the light fell in. But other than this, he gave absolutely no impression of having seen me at all. He lay back on that ice like a great cold queen on her throne and sighed, as though for luxury. I would have sworn it, but I don't swear by anything: and yet, I knew for certain he saw me.

He rubbed his back against the ice, and scratched his chest with a great hand. He sighed. "The hermit's hut gives lice and fleas."

Later, when I came to write about it in my diary, I started to liken him to a Viking barbarian king or chief because of his stature and power and the tattered things he was wearing. But that did not give the proper impression of his spirit. Certainly the flowing blond hair helped, but I suspected that his cold lack of attitude, lack of concern, and relentless self-assurance fostered the impression of queenliness. Draped over that ice like it was his natural bed, he spoke not to me but through me, so to speak. As though I had no existence. Maybe he spoke to himself. I had the distinct impression that he was all he needed, would always be there for himself, and that he really needed nothing. It was at once complete emptiness and self fulfillment.

Why have a bride then?

This thought slipped into my head as though I had no concern for anything else. That changed in less than an instant. This strangeness all happened in but an instant.

I thought, *What am I doing?* Mesmerized, I had wandered off into the woods. The flintlock musket grew heavier and heavier upon my back, recalling me to thought. I looked back and saw the icehouse down through the great boles of the trees.

I had seen the monster, the monster had seen me, and neither one of us showed it. Seeing him sitting there cool as you please, not acknowledging me in any way, I had simply closed the creaking door and walked off into the woods, leaving him in complete darkness.

I stood there looking back at the unobscured corner of the small log house, thinking.

He had seen the musket, surely. Surely he knew what it was. He would not have seen it on me before, either. His mention of the hermit's hut led me to believe that he'd been aware of my presence in the wilderness— perhaps even before I came upon Victor. *But why am I thinking about it?* This thing had surely killed Clairson, had threatened the life of Regina, of Victor's family, of Philippa, and was a threat to the whole community.... And yet he was a living being.

Or maybe partly alive. Was his a life in spirit? —Never had I felt more spiritual coldness from anything likely to be human. I laughed vaguely... nervy: *Likely to be human?* What does that mean?

Oh no, I thought. This won't do: I'm starting to question... my... what?— role as judge and executioner...? *Oh no.*

No no. I've got to kill him. *I've got to.* I went further away and found a rock to sit on, unslung the musket, the powder-horn, and the kit bag. As though to do so would stop all thought.

We had always called this father's flintlock. It was what he had killed with in the war. After, he had provided for us with it. But for this job I wished I had one of the new percussion guns they were talking of down in Farmington last time I was there. With that I'd be sure to hit my target without that target getting his hands on my throat first. There are so many things you have to get just right with this gun. You have to stay steady through the flash of the prime. That's not easy. But I was practiced, my lock was good, the flint sharp, the hammer not soft. You need to prime properly and have a well-placed touch hole. You want rapid ignition. The flint's got to strike right on the hammer. Oh, this thing is a beauty, a metalworking piece of art, wrought with curlicues, put together in fine. Try to lay eyes on one sometime. In fact there are hunters in the woods of your day using them when the regular deer season is over.

I pricked the touch hole to make sure it was clear.

The problem was that, in addition to attending to all this, I had to pay careful attention to the icehouse. The door opened onto the side facing down toward the river, and I was well behind in the trees. The trees were big and old, but leafless, and the woodland was thick with shadow from these big old boles and hightop conifers. Light from the opening river shone beyond.

I was still fumbling around in my mind with the question of whether or not I would actually kill him: That is, this was the underlayer of thought while careful attention was being paid to the works and the watch. Ramming powder and shot down into the barrel, I think I was praying under my breath, *Help me get him, help me get him.* When everything was ready, I moved quietly down below the icehouse, and sat behind a bole nearby. I pulled the brim of my hat low and peered past at the door. Still closed. I drew back and tipped a few grains of the powder-horn into the pan. The acrid smell of black powder came up to my face. I closed the hammer and cocked. As soon as the monster came out of that house, I was going to give fire. I was going to. *I was.*

I hunkered there, tense and waiting, listening. *When that door creaks....* Every so often I peered out, very wary. It would be better to hear the door opening than to give him sight of me again. I waited. I waited. Crouching so long started cramps in my legs: I stood and held the flintlock ready, pointing the muzzle at the thick bark, ready to sidestep the tree on hearing that door. The air was still, dry, and cool.

Reader, I stood there until the sun went low into the hills and twilight showed in the gapes around me. I was tense and exhausted – you cannot know. Then with trepidation I walked toward the ice house and lifted the latch.

You know he was gone.

I felt a deep relief, followed by remorse. Maybe I was not yet ready. Maybe I had wanted him to get away, had wanted him gone. But conscientiously I had gone through every motion to get him, and with great care. If it were meant it would have happened. I told myself this. But I thought, What am I to do?

If only the demented old man had been here in my stead, opening that door for me the first time... and if he had had my precision and strength. The one called himself Jasper, like the mountain. This flintlock had killed an enemy in a red coat for my father — not much older than me at the time—, how was I going to make it kill an avowed enemy?

An enemy who wants a bride for no good reason but mockery. The monster is pure and simple jealous of Victor and his good life, and wants but to mock it and him. What else is there for an ugly old mess like that but vindictiveness? He wants to capture satisfaction and thinks the bride will give it to him.

I turned away and trudged back down through the trees to the river. What do you want to think about that old thing and his motivation for?

I unrolled the blanket, wrapped myself up in it and fell asleep listening to the gentle rapids coming toward me on the curve of what was, to me, a very great river.

In my diary I stinted not displaying my perturbations and questions and troubles that beset me in this the ordeal. Since then, and handed down in town history, it made for good conversation between people of a thoughtful cast, and usually between all young people who heard the story. Young people really do love to think about all kinds of strange things, and to philosophize. Any stray wonderment coming into the mind they grasp hold of as though it were a part of themselves. Maybe thoughts just come to young people in order to get them to start thinking on their own. Of course the starting thoughts are not really their thoughts at all, but merely a starter, like yeast in the dough.

I'd say that Socrates may have felt this way about young people: look how all the Athenian youth gathered to him, in order to participate in thought. They were quite enamored of it, in part, because of his method. Of course, you can go overboard with that, as Paul saw their descendents doing in the *Book of Acts*. You can get stuck in the life of the mind, examining your life instead of actually living. Some of those Athenians just loved to get all wrapped up in rhetoric and strange ideas. This gave the apostle an opening more than once for that new thing, Christianity. The great thing about that book is that it is a combination of examining *and* living. Those first disciples sure knew how to live. And some of them knew how to write. I don't think you will catch God regretting having given *being* to them. That book is written in a very rational Greek style by the physician, possessing a beautiful rhythm combined of rhetoric and action, with a splendid touch of the Dionysian element which must accrue to every life. Take Victor's life. It combined both the rational and irrational, both self-examination and living, with a great deal of sensibility and passion... and, if he would but confess it (and I think he has), ignorance.

Greenleaf.

Tyger Tyger, burning bright,
*   In the forests of the night;*
*   What immortal hand or eye*
*   Could frame thy fearful symmetry?*
*   In what distant deeps or skies.*
*   Burnt the fire of thine eyes?*
*   On what wings dare he aspire?*
*   What the hand, dare seize the fire?*

These words came to me as I lay on my side looking out at the clean flowing Arossagunticook river, first light shining on its ruffled surface. The ground of the bank was dry, and I lay there on my blanket thinking of this poem of Blake's, comfortable but for the occasional itching. Yes, I was worshiping the Maker of the tiger, glad of the words of His poet that had come to help me do so.

*   When the stars threw down their spears*
*   And water'd heaven with their tears:*
*   Did he smile his work to see?*
*   Did he who made the Lamb make thee?*

I thought, The same hand made the unregenerate as made the Lamb. The thought of the tiger worried me not too much, for all his blazing brightness and ferocity: for he was nature. (There was a black panther up on the mountain equally ferocious so this was no rhetorical device for me.) And the Lamb I was thinking of was not the lamb in yonder pasture, but God as man.

How much, in his *Songs of Innocence and Experience*, the poet played upon the contrasting, the contrary, elements in our nature! And, I assume he thought, in God's. I was but eighteen and given such thoughts to think of late that I was near beset, but now I felt peaceable and at ease, and recognized in it grace. Grace. I thought about a certain form of duality, wheat and tares growing up together side-by-side, and thought I would have to let the same grow up in me until they might be parted at the great harvest.

Why can't I do it? Do I have to wait till his hands are on Regina? Why Lord?

The glorious great burning sun shone down the stretch of the river curving toward me. In the reddening trees above me a robin was singing its tender unmelodious song. *Is Victor going to make it? Or will he be destroyed?*

Grace.

What is the monster? He has being — his soul is there... I think. ...His psyche is after us to do its desire, that is a soul. I tried to look at him as the Greeks might, as I would look at a bit of poetry: What are his qualities?

What am I? We both have reason. He has the same passions... but not.... He doesn't care for the right things, except as they assuage himself. Goodness, love. They have no value independent of himself. No existence beyond that.

Why can't I?

You made me as you made me....

I would be satisfied with that, for now.

What am I? Sometimes I don't care for goodness and love independent of myself, either. I see in him the emotions, reason, perverted. Could I go that way? I thought about my lust for acceptance of my poetry growing side-by-side with the making of it. How many times had I been tempted to ask for an introduction to an editor of Dr. Kimball, our literary man whose articles on woodland Indians and wildlife appeared regularly in the Old World? I had not been able to conquer that. It *was*. Is. And sometimes the *not wanting* is too weak. Much too weak.

What am I?

I could not look at the sun between the dark clefts. It was too bright for my eyes. Fragile eyes in need of protection. I had to protect my eyes.

I had to protect a lot of my body. It might have died from any number of causes on Jasper Mountain. Anything at all could happen to it. Like this confounded lice. (I had been scratching away at it.)

Grace. This is grace. Lying here thinking, at peace. *You are*, I thought. I am (for you made me). You are because You are.

Grace permeated the mountains, their little hills, their trees with brown limbs swelling to red, here and there fuzzy with green. Grace permeated me. I was all grace. Now. You are. You are my soul's health. Wholesomeness. You. You. It was a whisper, like breathing. Like the veery thrush softly speaking, I breathed His name softly forth: *You. You. You.*

I woke again. "Abner, why did you leave? Why did you refuse Regina's hospitality? You did not eat her dinner."

I reached for the flintlock where it lay nigh on the bank. In its buckskin dressing it felt heavy, cold and thunderous. Sure. I pulled it in and sat up scratching, then rubbing my eyes. My mind flickered to its charge. Maybe it was too damp and I'd have to clean the barrel again. I also took in the condition of the day; morning, the sun just above the far mountain appearing at the end of the river's corner. Fine and dry. Were it to continue so, the field would be soon ready for the harrow.

"But I did not miss it: I took bread and tea. Had a nice meal out here. Got the cup here somewhere." I pawed among my belongings.

Victor stood impatiently a bit below on the bank. The river breeze rustled his dark hair. He was finely dressed in soft dove colored clothes, shivering a bit, his hands in his pockets. He had shaved, maybe again, his dimple neatly showing.

"He says you've got to get rid of the firearm."

Still sitting there in my blankets I stared at him.

"*He?*"

"*I* say. Abner you've got to trust me."

"Next you'll say, because you made him?"

"Abner. Listen to reason." His dark glance was as sharp as ever.

I would have said, *Reason got us into this*, but I wasn't quick.

"Eat something."

I looked and saw the covered dish he had brought with him there on the bank. Yes, I had been smelling the breakfast ever since he woke me. I guessed my stomach would work for him where reason wouldn't. Well, I would eat but be on my guard.

Sitting cross-legged, I lifted the clay lid. There was pork and beans and two withered apples. Heavenly. I began pitching it in. With my mouth full I looked at him over the edge of the pot and said, "He's bewitched you."

Victor said smartly, "I don't believe in it. This is not the dark ages, Abner."

"That's right, we are full of enlightenment and scientific understanding now. Even the mechanistic view is gone. Things are moved upon 'from a distance.' "

Remember, reader, at this stage in the evolution of humanism, we did not want to admit the irrational except as a kind of failing or intellectual sin. That changed when humanism understood that it *had* to incorporate it.

He was silent, looking at me with calculation. I could almost hear him thinking, You're not really trying to match wits with me, are you Abner?

He said, "Newton himself was divided in two. Don't be. Brilliant mathematician that he was, he did not seem to care how irrational this division was. His work moved God from the center to the periphery but he himself went along. You know that we have out-discovered, out-thought such forms. The enlightenment outgrew its Christian inception." He went on with this for a bit as, eating, I said nothing.

He stopped.

"You're getting nowhere with me: Why don't you try reasoning with *him*? Is he receptive to logic?" A bit of my meal spewed out in this relieving it, I thought, of much of its power. I knew I should slow down and either eat or talk but was both famished and too excited.

"Very good, Abner. You have the makings of a logician."

But I knew he *saw* my logic, not noticing the bits of pork and beans.

"Victor, why can't we go back to where we were in the beginning, when you were insistent that I slay the monster?" This was not meant to draw more logic, but simply as a reminder of how he had changed. The scientist was asserting himself again over the sufferer, in a true emblem of the age. "Do you remember that? When you understood that I would have a hard time killing him? We've covered a lot of wilderness on foot since, but it wasn't that long ago." I was astonished myself to think of all that had happened in so short a time. Was it really but days since my first seeing the white robin and Victor and nursing him?

"I am telling you, this is more and more like a bewitchment."

"That word is destroying your rhetorical power, Abner.... Will you take the gun back?... I do not want to do this, say this—. This is not to connive but warn, Abner. He has intimated to me that your mother may be needing it."

I stopped chewing. I set down the pot, and went to work gathering my things as tidily as possible, thoughtful and distracted, but with what I hoped was an appearance of deliberation. When my bedroll was tight and slung on my back, I picked up the musket and went up through the trees without looking back at him.

He had said nothing while I worked, but now he followed after me rustling through last year's fallen leaves. Although he knew exactly what I was about he said, "Return quickly. Our course has changed. I will be needing you in Bangor. He is going to follow us. With stealth. This he can manage quite easily.... And... if the alarm is raised while he is there,"—he had come rapidly up beside me, trying to read my countenance— "so much the better." His voice had lowered, and he said, "That may get rid of him for us."

"Secretly, without incrimination, you mean. That last part was a sop, Victor. Even if it *may* be your real hope. No, I will not be coming back here. I will be staying with mother: me and this flintlock!"

We walked rapidly across the stubbled field, Victor skipping to keep up. Then I stopped a moment.

"Victor, I know how your mother died.... I'm sorry." I said this gently then turned away to continue across lots. This stopped him a moment. And I may have said this thinking of my own mother. *At mother's, if he come, I will be able to kill him. I will.* But soon my thoughts were busy with something else, and since Victor continued with me again, but without speaking and perhaps trying to marshal his arguments, I said, "I don't understand why you fashioned him hideously as you did. Could you not have used one single body instead of the... well, what you *have* ?"

I half expected him to take up this question eagerly, but he said nothing at first. Then when he began to address it (as I thought), he stopped, giving curse under his breath. He said, "Here comes Greenleaf over the fields. Please say nothing."

I thought he wanted me to act nothing, as well. I managed to say, "Of course not." Yet I slowed my pace but a little. Long-legged youth, Greenleaf, was running, his coattails flapping.

"Victor! Victor!"

The sound of his calling came over the field to us, and soon he was with us. Victor stopped to speak to him, but I kept walking toward the road. *I will be able to do it now.*

"Victor, I want to help with the experiment! I want to learn from you!"

I checked my pace and glanced back, so as to listen. Greenleaf was maybe three years younger than I. He was also dark-haired, thin and a bit gangly, his wrists showing beneath the cuffs of his sleeves. His voice had not changed completely and he could not well modulate it. I heard him say, "I can assist you and Abner. I can help Abner gather and organize specimens."

I kept walking, and heard not what answer Victor made.

Specimens! But he must have lied to the boy. Probably told him I would be gathering herbs and things from the woodland and wayside. Or perhaps small animals, who knows? Then I was grumbling over that word *intimate*. The monster "*intimated*"? If Victor told me true, where does he get the subtlety? And his voice—so rich and powerful coupled with such naif innocence? Then Greenleaf was calling me, and I turned to see him running to catch up, Victor diminishing in the distance. He was going back toward the house.

Greenleaf was breathless. I stopped, puzzled and irritated. Victor was certainly trusting me —not to give him away... or to do anything at all to hurt his young brother. In part because of the so-prevalent death and dying in the District of Maine frontier, and in this era of but slowly evolving medical knowledge and healing arts, I knew the familial culture and that Victor would be a good and gentle older brother. *Perhaps not as watchful as he should be.* Especially not now with what he is about. I surmised him to be in just about the same state he was when he conceived and built the first monster, but perhaps with greater distraction being so near now to home and loved ones— the monster hovering.

"Good morning, Abner! Victor says I may come with you to run the errand to your house and gather things on the way back. I'm to tell you what is needed." With all this, to me, he seemed slightly disappointed and I guessed that he would rather be with his brother.... Doing important works that natural scientists do.

I was bemused and kept walking, but slower, not with brusqueness toward Greenleaf. I said nothing but let my thoughts stew themselves to some purpose, if they but would. I did not want him, but could think of no means right off to get rid of him. At last I said, "Why is Victor going home? I thought he was coming with me— us?" Not that I was going to believe whatever excuse he had given.

Greenleaf was almost as tall as myself and had no trouble keeping up as I took to the edges of the muddy rutted road leading back toward the village.

"He said he must pack and assemble his instruments and some books for the journey to Bangor. I want to go with him."

I looked at him sidelong, the crisp features of his profile made less attractive in his small chin. He had a dimple there, as did his brother, but not so deep. "What does he say to that?" I quickened my pace a bit.

"It... may take some convincing. ...I'm not daunted. I—even if I must go a bit after Victor."

Greatest of the Meguntic Mountains, Jasper Mountain's dark flank appeared to block the road ahead where it turned off into the village one way but proceeded around the other and along the river. His great bald head, now yet covered in winter white, was not in view for our nearness. I had known no one with time or inclination to make the summit in those days. I would have been exceedingly astonished, had I known that one of the owners of a burgeoning ski resort would stand in the winter blast, with Jim Nutting the newspaper editor, to look off at the great fulminating mass of black tires billowing ash and smoke and crusting the fire beneath, seemingly burning its way toward China. I had decided to avoid the village altogether and take the rough track into the woods behind it. This path would take me behind the pond as well and into the settlement of my birth. It was a bit longer, but I had no desire to meet anyone in the village this morning and was still trying to figure out how to send Greenleaf back home. I did not think he would be in any real danger of the monster at this time for Victor seemed acting toward him in good faith. In the meantime we kept to the road.

I remained taciturn and did not mind appearing a bit preoccupied, but Greenleaf kept up his talk cheerfully, looking out for things seen by the way; we would be needing mallow root, he said. Then he began remarking on this and that aspect of his brother's career, and the reading his brother had set him in mathematics and the natural sciences. Victor had steered him away from the philosophers. "He says I am not to read them much yet, but to learn all I can of nature and how she works. Malthus, Godwin, Galileo *On Motion*, Copernicus, *Opticks*,... oh! And he thinks I should read Gibbon."

How ironical, I thought. At the time I knew *of* the book but had not yet read it: *The Decline and Fall of the Roman Empire*. If you can't pick up the pattern of the great story there.... Well, the Bible has it as well, which is where I know it best, anyway. I gave a grunt here and there just to let him know I was listening as we tramped along through the played out weeds on the roadside. Then, nearing the village, we turned off, in the pathway I mentioned which followed the Kimball stone wall a ways.

We were well into the woods, the stone wall on our right hand so that we were on Dr. Kimball's land, Greenleaf still hopefully speaking of the wonders he had learned as we went. It was drier footing here, a common path used for this purpose and, for me, always a delightful woodland way. You could almost ever count on having it to yourself, for more sociable creatures preferred to pass through the village, if indeed they must pass at all. I loved the way the great strong limbs branched overhead, lacing, and in this season making a beautiful latticework upon the sky. It came to me then, what I should say. I slowed down a bit, the dressed flintlock still heavy in my hand.

"I... won't be coming back with you." I gave an apologetic glance and was about to say simply that I could not assist Victor but—

"He said you might not but asked —yes—told—me to come anyway. Will you tell me why? He did say you were troubled and that he is sorry— that *he* was the one who troubled you."

He seemed having a hard time bringing out the precise truth in his brother's sayings, but was managing it anyway. In a way he was being quite clear. I sensed that he lacked his brother's more direct manner and would rather be more delicate in his speech. I did not think long of this difference. Perhaps it was Regina's tender influence. By now we were far into the woods, away from the village and pond, and only just now turning back toward them again on their far side, leaving behind the stone wall.

His speaking relieved a great load for me, for I would not have lied, but also did not want to impugn Victor to his brother. Now I could see one or two of the rustic dwellings on our side of the pond through the trees, and noted smoke from chimneys pouring low. A storm was brewing, surely, somewhere not far distant the shore of the Gulf of Maine. All seemed fine this day, but the weather was breeding, a nor'easter maybe.

I did not answer, not tell him I thought this errand was to keep him out the way of Victor's journey to Bangor. "I think you had better go back," I said. This was not in warning of the storm which was still far out of range for his tramp. "But come home with me first and have a bite to eat, and let me speak with you a bit. I feel I must warn you that your household is in danger. Particularly Regina." This last came out almost of its own, and I was near as surprised as Greenleaf to hear it. Surely I should have waited until we were comfortable at home, and giving it a better approach. But there it was.

Instantly he said, "Victor would not allow that. Victor would say, if it were so.... What can you mean, Abner?"

I was surprised at the sternness in his cracking voice, which had no native quality of sternness in and of itself. It was his heart in it that made me feel strength.

"I'm sorry. I will say no more. But I want you to take a weapon on your way home with you—and keep it. I will find something. Maybe the hatchet, something for you to keep by you should you need it." But then I wondered about that hatchet: surely Greenleaf would not be practiced enough with it.

"Abner! I'm sure I shall not need it!"

I had made an awful blunder. Now what was I to do?

"Greenleaf, I—. You love your brother."

"Yes! I love Victor. He is everything! He would not allow jeopardy of us if he knew aught. You imply great wrong. Please retract it!" In his fresh face was all the outrage and surprise he felt that another could think ill of his brother.

"I can't."

He stared at me bright-faced one instant, then turned and went back down the path. I stood watching his retreat, small brown figure beneath the great trees. He never looked back.

Cannot be helped. And now he will watch. I felt lighter, and continued on my way home.

In the Cellar

I was asleep when I heard them knocking then banging on the door. Mother was calling to me. Somehow I was off my pallet and had climbed into my clothes, hopping, one foot at a time. But already they were stomping into the house and up the stairs. Some guard, I thought of myself, scornfully. The monster could be sitting down to supper. They grabbed me and roughly hustled me down the ladder. There was but the one candle with them, and it cast more shadow than light. I did not fully realize what was happening until we were out the door, and I glanced back to see Mother, dark, backlit against the candlelight in the kitchen. She had not said a word. I was too harassed to think what she might do on my behalf but only of what must have been her bewilderment.

It was night, cold, the wind blowing, storm-making; limbs overhead creaking, cracking, and occasionally dropping. I stumbled along between them in the dark trying to snatch breath, asking questions, and getting rough answers, answers I could scarcely credit. Yes, I recognized the two fellows, the burliest men in Gott'im, Haminiah Bean and Gus, for Augustus, Kimball. I struggled between them, just wanting to be let loose to walk on my own, and protesting every moment. "I had nothing to do with it!" I said this over several times. I hollered, furious. "I could tell you who did! I could tell you who did!"

"Young man, tell it to the deputy sheriff when he gets here!" Gus Kimball said it harshly. I struggled mightily, hollering, but they picked me up between them—I was nought but skin and bone from my privations and exertions. Ham Bean tightened his grip and brought my arm back behind me so high I could but have grabbed my ear. I pleaded with him to relax it and promised to come with them quietly. He did, a very little, but swore he would boot my butt up between my shoulder blades if I didn't behave. We went round the pond like this, and then I saw folks lining School Street in the dark, not like you'd see in the shire town Farmington, but enough to let me know 'twas the whole village. There I was, tossed along in the breeze between the two rough fellows, and humiliated past despair.

But Greenleaf was killed.

I was accused of his murder.

I was to spend the rest of the night shivering in the rootcellar at Dr. Kimball's, locked in the dark and dank with but a blanket, while the storm banged; huddling in the corner among the rubble between walls of hewn granite stone. Above me the stout door at the top of the stairs was barred and guarded. I was to be fetched away on the morrow to the stone jail in the shire town. Victor will come, I thought. Even though his brother is dead, *he will not forget me.*

You think despair is a silent thing, draining the life away, wearying. No, despair is a boiling thing, an emotion of tumult, driving the mind thither and yon. One moment I was thinking with horror of slim young Greenleaf in the great hands of the monster, the next numbly contemplating the irony of my stay in the cellar as monster of the community of Gott'im. Didn't the monster live in the cellar, I idly wondered before being shaken again in the realization of Greenleaf's brutal passing. *Oh that innocent beautiful pathway between the Twombly Road and the hamlet! Oh, you'll never be the same again, never. There is blood there now. Blood calling out!* I am Dr. Kimball's latest greatest curiosity, displayed in his cellar for the lawman of the District of Maine. *Oh! I am a monster, letting Greenleaf go like that when I <u>knew</u> he was in danger.*

Shivering, trembling. *Darkness.* I could see nothing, losing the sense of my body and person, the dimensions of my being. I felt for something that seemed like my arm. It was not my arm, not where it belonged, attached to me. I felt for my knees. They were not my knees. Disembodied, made up of parts not my own. I was become darkness and trembling. *Void. How long?* When will Victor come? Victor, Victor, you are. *I will fear no evil.*

This is not dreamed. Not dreamed. *Shivering.* Have they taken me from my bed? Am I still in my bed but dreaming this awful thing?

Shivering, trembling.

At last I became aware of something else beside the awful darkness and cold, the dankness and trembling, my running nose. I began to feel the discomfort of the things upon which I was sitting, but also I heard the sounds. The sound of the wind thrashing the house, with creakings and shivering. The blast was thrashing the village of Gott'im as I sat down here in the corner shivering.

Merciful merciful. Mercy mercy. I trembled, huddling in the roots and rocks. The wind above howled its breathful roaring and scraping. I could hear nothing but the wind, and its way with the house and throughout the pitiful few lanes of the village. It had come down with great violence from Jasper Mountain where it held its continual sway between the stars.

Victor can't come, he's dressing his brother's body for the burial. I will fear no evil.

Victor can't think of me, may not even know about me, how can they think I would murder his brother? Victor is worried about the monster getting Regina and his father. Why would the monster do this? When he had Victor in his will? There is no reason! No reason!

There is no rhyme in this, either. It breaks the entire pattern, fits no rational purpose.

Shivering. The void. Is this Dr. Kimball's cellar?

Why did I let Greenleaf go?

Greenleaf. Victor's dear young brother.

I began coughing and sneezing. I don't know how long I hunched there, my thought sinking low in growing numbness and bodily helpless trembling. Then pale lines high above, suggestions of feeble light, began showing in the darkness, and I realized that Gottheim had turned toward the sun just a bit more, it yet beneath the horizon and but faintly showing forth the cracks in the foundation between its great hewn granite-stones and its floorplates above.

The door to the upper part opened and candlelight shone round the great dark forms of my jailers. Ham Bean called to me, his harsh voice like a beacon. I did not have to be told twice to get up the steps, but I could not move. Next I knew they had their hands on me, dragging me forth and up steps where my feet could not move me. They pulled me, blinking, this way and that until finally we were in the kitchen of the house, and Doctor Kimball there seated, his shining spectacles lying on the table between his fingers momently at rest. He wore his gray hair pulled back in a tail like our fathers, and the glance in his eye was very solemn indeed. Candlelight gleamed on his high bald pate.

They sat me in a bowed-back chair at the table, and I felt my fingers numbly grab to pull the blanket closer. The hearth fire was blazing beneath the mantelpiece lined with fine things and there was a great mug of something— spiced cider? "Drink that, young man," said Dr. Kimball. "Drink that and stop coughing. Get that into you and let the fire warm you and stimulate your mind."

I pulled the mug slowly toward me but could scarcely lift it. I lowered my head and shifted its nourishing warmth into me. So hot and good. I wiped my nose.

He had turned his attention to the burly men behind me. I heard him say something to them, and their answer, but do not recall what it was.

I drank it down. He pointed out bread and butter. I ate them.

He said, "Do not worry, Abner. I trust you did no such thing. I know you too well for that. You know Gottheim. Here you cannot go off and leave your mother to work the farmstead alone for the sake of your idle dreaming without harm to your reputation. They have thought, He is feckless and irresponsible and up to no good going off there like that for no reason." He glanced sharply up behind me at the two men. I felt them shift on the punkin pine floor behind me, saw their great arms akimbo move, out the corner of my eye.

"Add to that the fact that you were seen with young Greenleaf going into the woods, and not long after he was found lying up there among the leafmould, the thumb print of his agony still in his throat:... They have their culprit. I'm sorry." He reached out his stout hand and gripped my yet trembling arm. "It will be all right. It will be all right, Abner."

Above me Augustus Kimball said, "I hope you realize the goodness my kinsman has shown you— in vouchsafing you like this."

Dr. Kimball looked apologetically at me. "I'm sorry it took so long to get you from the cellar. These good men had to be convinced." He seemed to want to impress me with their goodness. They shifted again behind me. Probably embarrassed—at the least. He looked up at them again. "Please sit down, good men."

They refused. My voice croaked. "The monster is still out there," I said. "There may be more dead—Besiegt." I wiped my nose.

There was silence. Dr. Kimball looked up at the two men and back at me. "Monster, you say?" He was doubtful.

I sensed the deep skepticism and... something else in the room. But his expression was kindly.

How to begin? I felt so here-and-there, my wits scarcely working despite the hard cider. I felt a bit wobbly, still shivering. Yesterday — was it only yesterday?—while Greenleaf was still alive! —I had come home and started right away doing things needing done as my mother prepared the fomentation of cider vinegar and butternut husk tea to kill every louse upon me. When I had eaten, bathed and washed all my clothes and hung them out to dry, I tumbled into bed. The broadsheet with the conjoined twins had to be destroyed in the fire. Now as I sat here dazed and still shivering, my eye fell upon another of the selfsame broadsheet, showing the Siamese twins, on the table near to his hand.

"There! There! The monster." I reached out and nudged it closer him. "Victor's monster," I said. "It followed him here from Cambridge. The monster killed Greenleaf. It doesn't make sense why, but mostly jealousy, wouldn't you say?" I shivered and took another warming swallow.

The men back of me shifted uneasily, and, if anything, the look in the doctor's eye grew more kindly. Above my left ear, Augustus said, "They said nothin' bout needing any help when they came'n took Greenleaf's body home on a plank, their men did." It came out in a hurry, as though he were trying to smooth over my crazy talk with something reasonable. I felt helpless, unable to describe any of what I had been —*we* had been through. The two men had stepped back just a bit and were become restive.

Dimly I thought, *Now they're afraid of me.* Desperately I said, "Don't you see? They can't get rid of each other. —Victor and the monster — it's like they're tied together. And God has got to separate them! I tried but I can't."

I let go the tankard and sat there clenching and unclenching my hands on the table. A log fell low in the grate and the blaze caught my eye a moment. The silence deepened then. I slouched there in the blanket sniffling, and now looked up into Dr. Kimball's eye and saw him regarding me with care. I heard a movement in the next room, and one softly hush another. I tried to look back but Ham Bean blocked my view of the dining room. I thought 'twas the dining room.

Dr. Kimball said, "We have heard his mother. She knew nothing of this... which makes me believe there *may* be some truth in it." He was looking from one to another, and raised his voice a bit. "I wouldn't be too concerned, considering what he endured in the cellar.... for so long."

Again the men shifted. Ham Bean said, "*That* can't be right, those things. That is not a right mind."

"Neither is spending the night in a dark root cellar conducive to sanity."

Dawn was spreading a golden light outside the divided panes of the window, but now a movement caught my eye there, and I saw beyond the porch support, her: all cloaked, pale and serene on a white mare. Horse and rider were crossing the pale greening yard a'sparkle with raindrops, Regina's aproned skirt spread over its flank. Oh, she was like every beautiful woman-thing God had ever made. She was all of them in one. My breath was caught. Tears watered my eyes.

"He must not get her." I whispered it. "The monster *it-must-not* get her." I said it aloud.

Dr. Kimball had turned and seen her as well; and now he stood, scraping back his chair, saying, "Stay with him —gently— till I return."

I did not care. I drank the cider. I felt a small gain. I said into the mug, "I forgive your rough handling the last night." I knew it would make them mad but I didn't care.

"Yes. Well, thank you," said Augustus, still uneasy.

Ham Bean said nothing and I sensed the deep glare he sent into my backside.

Before long Dr. Kimball was back. Through the divided lights I saw Regina and the mare pass back over the yard. He seated himself in his chair at table saying, "It is as his mother has said. This youth is innocent of any crime. Regina has saving news. You may go."

I turned to look in time to catch the incredulity of their rugged but stupid faces. Ham Bean with his big nose looked angry, and Augustus beneath his pink balding head seemed relieved. But I sensed their reluctance to quit the place, that curiosity had taken over and now they just *had* to know what would come of it. *If he's not crazy—then what?* And, *What is going on at Besiegt's?*

I did not resist saying, "We may need you yet, sirs, to help with the monster." I upended the tankard and swallowed the last of the cider. When I looked back to say further that they should follow Regina, they had gone. And I saw straight into the room, and there sat Mother and Philippa by the window. I started.

They stood and came toward me, mother all solemn, dark salt-and-pepper curls straying from her dingy mobcap. I was not even embarrassed that she had on father's old hunting frock. Philippa shone with strong joy in her face. Her white cap was low back on her darkly golden head, her apron almost as bright as Regina's. She stooped and hugged me. She had not done so since I was but a toddling scamp. There are no great shows of affection among us in Gott'im. I looked down, embarrassed but pleased. Dr. Kimball stood and invited them to sit down.

The woman came and began steeping tea from the kettle on the hob, and dishing up cornbread from the larder. She worked away and before long I was also smelling bacon, but I had already put away three junks of thickly buttered cornbread. I paid more attention to eating than I did to the conversation that followed. Low golden light was streaming in and bright patches appeared on the dresser, cupboards and sideboard. The good smell grew bigger and bigger in the room, and, drinking the hot tea, I seemed to expand right along with it. The warmth was big all through me.

But when the meal was over and I stood to go, it was with new understanding. It seems that some sort of thug, some extortioner, had followed Victor up from the big city and would not leave him be. When Victor refused to submit, this dastard killed his brother in a cowardly rage.

I guess you can see why I paid no mind, it's being cooked up by Victor, who was himself turning out to be something of the dastard, for purposes of denying the monster's existence, I guessed. *Or, if I wanted to be kind,* I thought, I might just say perhaps he thought no one would believe him: You made a monster out of dead people and now he's walking around killing your relatives? Grudgingly, I had to grant him a point.

I stepped off the porch into the wet grass with my mother and sister on either arm. The doctor, standing above us, said "I am sure the deputy will want to speak to you when he gets here." And then, in that moment more gratifyingly than anything I should admit to, he said, "And perhaps we can have a little conversation ourselves sometime. Shall we?" His face seemed quite solemn at this, but for a moment I thought I saw a twinkle somewhere. Maybe not, but immediately I thought of my journal.... still in one of my pouches, up in my room under the eave. *That* I would never burn. *Abner, Abner, fishing again.* I shook my head. Probably wants to examine me as a curio.

We had not gone far toward the Common, where the neighborhood cows were just beginning to graze a few new sprouts, when 'twas discovered that Abner Bartlett was no more the grist for gossip but Victor Besiegt was on every tongue.

What can it mean? What can Victor have done to draw such malevolent attention? Why would he need to pay money? What kind of trouble can he have got himself in, such a studious, intelligent, high-minded man as that? And of course, "What do you know of the matter, Abner?"

Weren't you one who stood at this side the street and watched me pass Melville's store between them last night, Miz Rowe? But I said nothing, only stared at her and she took the hint and looked away. Yes, I'll admit without excuse: Big of me, was it not?

I relented and said, "How're those new red hens fom down't Guildfid way, Miz Rowe?"

You may wonder at Regina's coming with the message that set me free. In those days, still, you might find the men washing and laying out their own sex for the burying. But yet I imagine her grief over the one she had raised when she herself was most a child. And to come any how to my aid. But — it was not in aid of me as Abner, but me as a neighbor and body needing justice and mercy despite the storm of worry and grief.

I could not think how they let her come, knowing the danger. Had Victor told them of the monster? *At least*, I thought, *the horse would run her away at his approach*. There was my only consoling hope.

She had handed me my pouch, and I had warned mother with great emphasis to fetch our weapons and stay at Philippa's but she refused. She would however ascertain the state of the weapons in both households, including father's musket, and promised to stand guard and do father proud should the villain approach. They did not need to say that Philippa's husband Franklin was with the children even now. But mother would not let me go right off. For the first time I noticed how her face was aging, and there being almost more gray among the black of her curls. In the light of day, fine wrinkles etched her face all over; and her skin looked dry and white. Her dark eyes on me were troublous, but of this she said nothing. Dryly she put it. "So, feckless and unprofitable youth, you leave me again to the rock picking, field dressing, cow, pig and sheep tending. You know we got to get those bodies sheared."

"I know that they will wait. But that household needs me now, mother. I do not think he will come to the Bartlett's. I tell you it *is* a monster. He has showed his unreasoning, but I think it all pertains to his maker."

"Last time I saw the young man in question, there was but the one of him to a set of legs." (Drier than kindling in February.) She was thinking, This must be another one of your poetic flights, Abner.

But she let me go, and I was with Victor at the Besiegt household again, this time conferring with him in the dooryard by the lane. Family and friends would be attending soon, and Greenleaf to be laid in the family burying ground.

He said, "Please accept my apologies for leaving you as I did, Abner." He gazed at me intently, solemnly. "It might have been you. Even now I cannot wish that it had been. It should have been, it *must* have been, me. We know it. *Why? Why?* He makes no sense to me. Do you know they called me back from the road to Bangor? I was doing everything. Everything he wanted."

I looked at him. "Ever hear of jealousy? He told you. *Clairson.* There is no reason to that. Envy needs no reason, I'm learning, from your... progeny." The child of your applied scientific rational philosophy, I thought but did not say it. Even the other should not have been said.

"—I'm sorry. No! I should have saved Greenleaf, Victor. *I* knew he was in danger. You still believed in—him."

He shook his head, but let it go. "We have other things to discuss now."

"But why did you let Regina go off alone to fetch me— after?"

"We—father and I were—with Greenleaf. —I did not know what she was about."

Suddenly, for the first time since I saw Victor beneath the white robin and roused him to usefulness, he was sunken. Abject. But silently so. He stared at the ground. I looked toward the house where some of its upper divided lights showed back the blue sky.

He said, "Without you here... Abner it was everything I possessed of faculty to stay with Father, and prepare—for the burying.... He was so young. So young.... So hopeful. So *alive.* He loved me so much.... I wanted to run off again."

He looked up at me. "Yes. You did know. I *was* running from him. When I saw you I revived: You, the pioneer youth, were going to kill the monster. You should have left me there. Greenleaf would still *be.*" He said the last word with vehemence.

"Victor," I said, "quit your despondence now. *Now!* Victor. Quit it!"

He looked at me. I was relieved to see the suggestion of his former sharpness in his dark eyes. His face was ghastly, the eyes protuberant, his skull manifest beneath the taut skin by the deep physical and mental distress he labored under. He blinked.

I heard horse hooves hitting the lane behind me before he noticed the approach he was facing. I turned. The great horse and rider came steadily toward us, dressed in buckskin and canvas. He was great of build, masterfully proportioned, taller than anybody I had ever seen except the monster. His saddle bags were of tarpaulin canvas, stitched and pine-tarred by hand. It had to be *Lewis Loomis!* —great woodsman and hunter, pioneer lawman, *and* had apprehended the infamous kidnapper, Robin David, *without the aid of a posse*; denying its efficacy in such a pursuit through all kinds of terrain and waters from Farmington through to the disputed Canadian border.

Joy and hope pushed up in me like sap rising in late February. *This! This lawman,* I thought. He is the man to get *the monster.* I would have gone down on my knees in thanksgiving to the great Lord... but that would have been embarrassing.... It did cross my mind that this failure would occasion the Lord to be embarrassed by me at the judgment — but I had to let it pass. The monster was done for! Regina was saved! The Besiegts were going to live again! And Gott'im would be safe in its insular small-mindedness and uneasy communal harmonics for ever. Mother would learn all about it and be well. I would make a master-smart epic poem and rank with Blake and Burns!— That last was questionable but present nonetheless. All flashed in my mind like sudden sun on the Rossy River, when I saw and realized Lewis Loomis was here.

Mr. Loomis swung off his great mount and came toward us where we stood in the dooryard away from the house. The lilac shrubbery was red of twig and incipient budding, tall and plentiful about the lane in the approach to the house. There chickadees twittered and hopped, waiting the final gathering and push of the mighty northern spring. It can happen here in a single day, for our calendar is lengthy with chill, wind, snow and mud as the thaw comes slowly out of the earth and releases her from the toils of long bitter winter.

"Lewis Loomis, deputy fom Fahminton," he said, with a reverse nod. Had I been a Southerner from Carolina, what with my feeling and rejoicing within, I'd have grabbed his hand and pumped it, grinning. As it was I but nodded. No smile. Victor said, with perceptible effort, "How do you do? This is Abner Bartlett. I am Victor Besiegt and responsible for the death of my young brother Greenleaf."

Mr. Loomis towered ponderously over the both of us. Having dismissed me from view, he looked at Victor, digging in his pocket. He came up with a duck-bound notebook, one I could not take my eyes off for envy, opened it, and said, "I understand this man followed you home here from Boston?" He looked again and said, "Cambridge."

Victor started right off evasive. I had to restrain myself severely. He said, "Thereabout."

"Why?" Loomis had a massive neck, broad jaw and plentiful hair, close-cropped as we reckoned it in those days; just fringing over his brown twill collar.

Victor blinked. The deputy noticed. The young scholar of the city expecting deference, no doubt. "The usual thuggery," said that one, his old sharpness waxing now. He slipped his hands into the pockets of his breeches and set back a bit on his heels.

Loomis looked at him. He chewed a bit on the wad in his cheek and spat a string of brown juice into the base of a nearby lilac. The chickadees fluttered up a bit higher among the twigs.

"He... was trying to extort a sum of money."

"For? And how much? What was his name?" Loomis might ask a trio of questions, but he always came back for all the answers eventually. He shifted the wad to the right cheek.

"Oh, any amount he could obtain, I supposed. I had no interest in dealing with him, one Alfeus Jones. Tried to brush him off. — It was — a mistake, as you see. I should have given him money. I wish I had." He looked away.

Loomis was still, even his jaw. Then he said, "I have to ask you again...."

Without looking back at him, Victor said, "Because I was robbing graves for my medical studies and he was helping me. He thought the wages of blackmail better pay, perhaps."

This was as cool and heavy as pond water just before the frost. I shook my head in disgust. The famous Loomis glanced at me, then back. He may have mistaken my gesture as applying to the practice of vivisection and grave defilement. I shifted impatiently but said nothing, a complete show of self containment and maturity... anybody could see it.

The deputy worked his wad and spat again. He jotted something with his graphite stylus, a pencil I think 'twas, which also excited my envy. But then he asked the question I had been waiting for. "How do you know it was him? And what does he looked like?"

"No one else it could have been. He's been to see me. Abner here saved me in the woods when I was running away from him. He can testify to my condition. I had drawn him off my family but, if you want to know, I was afraid. I've seen what he can do. He killed Henry Clairson in Cambridge. Drowned him in the Charles. —I heard."

"You heard?" He let it pass, but would surely come back to it. He made another note, and said, "What's he look like?"

"Big, disheveled, dressed in smallish rags, probably stolen from some clothesline. Has a cut on his face. Several cuts. You will say, when you see him, that's him." Victor looked at me. "The type of brute thug, Mr. Loomis," he said.

Lewis Loomis looked at him, considering. He now had time for me. He turned and said, "Abnah Bahlett. You're one they thought done it?"

"At first."

"When did you see him? Was the young man present?"

"No. He was in the icehouse—day before yestadee 'twas. Next day Greenleaf and I were going to my cabin behind the pond on an errand for Victor. Supposedly." I thought I could not help adding the last.

Loomis look surprised: I did not think it possible. "The icehouse?"

"Sat there on the ice like it was pleasant."

He looked ruminative, doubtful. "Why there? How'd you happen to see this? What did he do when he saw you?"

"Nothing."

Loomis looked at me. His eyes, brows, and hair were all the same color, a bit sere, like old leaves. "What did he look like?" This was the question he most wanted to get at. There must be no mistake at capture. For my own reasons, I thought it his most important question.

Victor intervened. "My description of him is as complete as it can be for your purposes. I will testify to it when you've captured him." He said this in an almost offhand manner.

I said, "He has long yellow hair like a woman's, yellow-black eyes, greenish skin, big strange joints, and is scarred all over where he's been sewed together from other people... every part of him. Practically."

Mr. Loomis stopped writing. He looked at me. Then he turned back through his notes, seemed to draw a conclusion, closed the book and said, "Any idea where he went? Back to Cambridge, Québec, the Aroostook?" He was looking at Victor.

My elation over his coming sank into its opposite. I was soaked in disappointment, but saw it all: My answer, coupled with the observations of Ham Bean and others, even probably Dr. Kimball, proved the conclusion.

As he was leaving, mounted on his great horse, I called after him "He'll be staying around, maybe on Jaspa Mountain, he'll still be wanting Victor to make him a bride from cadavers!"

When he was gone, Victor looked at me.

"It was the truth," I said. "Should I lie? How does it help, either?"

"If he sees the monster, he'll know all. And if not I will not have to face my father with what I have done to him with my—*monster*."

He turned and went back toward the house through the stems of lilac where the lane curved through. He turned back, the breeze ruffling his dark hair. "Abner. I need you to kill him. I do."

Starlight sparkled in the dark sky through stiff branches. We stood in the dark below Regina's upstairs window, quietly talking as we stood the watch. Rather, Victor talked. I listened and thought my own thoughts. The ground sloped ever so slightly down toward the river out of sight in the woods. I watched, turning slowly about as softly he continued.

"As a poet you rightly subsumed the strictly rational, putting it in its appropriate place—where the craft resides. Clairson and I talked of this. I think now he has helped me— too late —helped me see my delusion that purely rational, mathematical, and mechanistic methodology is but that —a method not to be confused with what I am. People are not rational —methods may be. Classification is, science, specialization, studies. If we will work toward the objective we will do well in our work, but we are mistaken to think ourselves and our motives as good as our studies."

We stood watching together. I leaned against the house, my glance always on the move through the trees; but occasionally, when I could not help I glanced at the window above, let gaze drift up toward starlight. How it spangled all the branches. *Oh.*

"Pascal knew this," he quietly said. "But he could never have been a deist as he thought Descartes, who would only allow that God nudged the whole of being into existence and went off somewhere... to wrap himself up in a rose... or some thing. Pascal knew that we are irrational. I grant that I'm a contradiction in terms (and suffer for it) but this is reason the more to think we are left to ourselves. The whole of mankind is so. And, by the way, why shouldn't we believe God irrational also, if, as you believe, we are made in his image? Look. Say he has used great—astounding—craft to bring it all about, and that old work keeps it, and us, going. Craft *must* be rational to make all this. But your God is as hopeless as we are."

By way of analogy, drawing parallels all the while, Victor told me of the few first shocking impressions he had of the monster on seeing him near here after the breakup at Griswold's. Victor made a clean breast of all to me (owing for some time, I thought), and continued to draw parallels with what God "had done" in conceiving this great creation and imbuing it, as a baby would, with futile fantasies of what he might expect from it all.

I could not help chuckling. "So God, now, is at fault?"

"Why, if he is omnipotent, didn't he stop me? Or why the necessity of the French Reign of Terror? Why the entire history of these empires, Egyptian, Greek, Babylonian, Roman, Napoleon et al., with their pathetic ends and vulgar decadence? ...Greenleaf.... You see—it's not that he is at fault, as you put it, but must be incapable, as I am, of righting this terrible wrong. A *fault* (by such as him) might signify something rightable. This clearly is not. We continue as always — no matter the ideal of progress. It is mistaken. We remain unchanged, if our craft progress."

I said quietly, "What is your monster thinking of now? Is he waiting for you to stop him from killing—." I should not have gone on with it. Not with the painful lesson of Greenleaf haunting our every thought. "All he can do is think, *Kill Victor's lovers*, and *How can I get Victor to do whatever I want?* You were at least thinking, *How can I help others live long?* Mightn't God think of that, too, and not the other?"

After a moment he made quiet, honest response. "Ah, Abner. But we do know, from history and the broadsheet, that there are those among us who think like my —the monster. Is that the image of God? Or how, if it's not, can it *be, at all*, if all is made by God—even that other spirit we are taught fell from heaven. How can there be a fall if all are come out of his thought, and he is good?" All his points were quietly put.

I was stumped. He had me. I stood staring at him in the lamplight cutting the dark and showing his face now shaded in profile. I said quietly, "That's what the lesson of the Garden is for— free will —the coming savior, the crucifixion. The resurrection and redemption." I felt I was parroting the catechism in the face of tragedy; and Greenleaf's lying in his coffin in the parlor, his father by his side. I willed it to, but how could it possibly help?

He was silent. I saw his dark glance going to and fro, carefully; watching the trees. He whispered to me again. "You know, I've thought about the story. I don't believe it was paradise because they need only reach out a hand to eat. Or because they wore no clothes and were free of convention. Or even because they were innocent. We would be too restless after a bit and need that fruit to upset the applecart." He laughed a bit over the pun, softly wretched. But I noticed there was no bitterness in it. Bitterness. It was missing from Victor's tone tonight—as though it were no longer part of the rough music coming out of the being of Victor Besiegt. Quietly he said, "No. It was paradise because...." He waited, as though for me to see it.

I could think of nothing.

Then it was there.

I said, "Because He was there."

"Yes. He was talking to them. Even as you and I talk. He was their visiting friend. In that story, every day."

Silence came. Regina was upstairs, her lamplight glowed softly out on a patch of trees in God's wilderness. In the room behind us, its glazed windows slightly above our heads to the left, the elder Dr. Besiegt was sitting beside the body of his young son. Soon the two mourners would meet and change the watch. Silence was with us. Even the river made a small silence far below us. I heard the wind on Jasper

Mountain, distant, high. Silence, full of stars, full of quiet questions. And mourning.

Victor anticipated my reiteration and said, "It would not be the same. That resurrection of yours. Think of it. It cannot be rational to expect Christ to be with each of us, Abner. You say 'the hairs of our heads are numbered,' but that is not the same as person-to-person... as we are here talking. How can it be? When there are hundreds of millions of us by this time? Did I tell you about Malthus's theorem, by the way? Can He even feed us all let alone speak to each?"

I was silent, then said, "I don't know about them—how can I? How can I care?... I care about Mother, my sister. Gott'im, sometimes." I tried again. "Who said all men are brothers?"

"Yes, 'Then all wars are civil wars,'... François Fénelon and the Quietist Movement."

"Then they must have one father. Can adaptability be a father to us? Fatherhood is his responsibility for us, even to the feeding of us. I know what I experience, Victor."

"You're saying, Him?"

"Yes."

He was silent, looking at me, I thought. I was looking at the stars, but then I looked him back.

"You believe this?"

"Yes." I said it very softly.

He was still looking at me. Regina's light went out. Now there was less for us here below the stars. Only a very subdued light remained, from the candle in the parlor where Victor's father watched. You are likely wondering why we waited by the open coffin of our loved ones whom we ourselves had washed and dressed in simple shrouds. We needed to be certain of death. The body continuing rigid with its ways in death—well, we did not want to make a mistake. On feeling the stiffness we were sure. It was empty. And then 'twas time to bestow it to the ground that had nourished it, its turn now to nourish ground.

"Victor. You recall saying you felt a sense, a kind of touch, or maybe 'twas a pressure, very slight... not to give power to the thing you had — made?"

He said nothing. And I could not make out his face.

Then I felt him turn away. I heard him murmur. "Yes. I have thought as much."

The moment passed. The light in the parlor grew a bit. Victor said, "She is with him now."

Stepping past, he brushed against me. "I'll go stand a bit with them. I can see Greenleaf yet again. ...Now. Will you walk about a bit? The others will see to it here." He meant the men, workers of the household. "Or will you go in and sleep? Take my room. I've had snatches of rest this awful day—I think—anyway, I cannot sleep."

Notwithstanding that I had had small snatches of it myself, I said, "I will walk."

I had followed with him as we turned the corner, but started now toward the river. He called me back, and we met partway, still in the trees.

Very low he said, "I will not dispute the touch I had, reason it away, or say I imagined it. ...I still wish he had taken hold of my hand, appeared, said *Do not do this*. Or even, outraged, beat me up."

I thought a moment. "I do not think it is his way. Not now."

He did not ask me what I meant by that last. He stood thoughtful a moment. Then he went away. I watched him disappear in darkness. He must've turned the corner, I could not tell. As I went down among the dark trunks I might have thought it a good prospect that Victor had not asked me what I meant by the *Not now*. If he had, and I had been older, I might have been tempted to think perhaps he was simply following again his curiosity and leaving the better part untouched. That maybe I still did not know what kind of ground that seed would be given, and that he was but checked by grief and all his natural man would reassert itself again. The rational Christian, me? But I did not think of it. I was eighteen years old: I felt myself walking toward the stars up in the branches. The joyful stars, God going out to *get* glory in his own irrational way.

Watching the graveside group gather in morning light, at a distance, I stood on the edge of the woods upriver. Watching with me were other villagers, scattered among the trees, Lewis Loomis among them. I still did not think I would — or could — kill him. But I could stand guard until Loomis caught him. I could guard the household in their grief, or in their daily work. A chill breeze penetrated my homespun and buckskin. Dr. Besiegt had given me the flintlock he lends to the men to get deer, and I stood with my legs apart, the butt of the musket resting on the ground. Its muzzle was almost up to my chin. Remembering something from my past adventures, I had in my belt a hatchet borrowed of Mrs. Crockett's son, William, also my friend. And he was one of the bearers.

Everyone in Gottheim thereabouts was with them, nearly 200 souls. To the delicate sounds of the fife helping its bearers keep step, the body, in its peculiar box, came through the orchard toward the family burying ground. Victor was among them, at the right fore. He was dressed in dark charcoal, a band of black on his upper arm, barely distinguishable. Or maybe I *knew* it was there and did not really see it, remote as I was. I had not been to the house for the simple ceremony.

Later I went back to read the record of what Dr. Besiegt had said during that ceremony. It is a bit like time-travel: Reading the record in the archives of heaven means seeing the experience, even of others, again... and hearing their words, how it all looked and smelled, what were their thoughts and feelings; all the particulars of existence... without being able to change a thing.

The house was full, folks even standing at doors and open windows, the cold notwithstanding, to give listen to the words of Dr. Besiegt. Greenleaf, his features crisp but waxen, lay still in the open pine coffin made by Phineas Rowe, a man about the place; flanked with pots of dried tansy all yellow and green— as it had been saved in the dark of many a community attic for just such a purpose, and rosemary was also on hand. Regina, Victor and Greenleaf's father, sat nigh; and the community members came in, coming forward a few at a time, quietly offering their condolences. The looking glass and pictures throughout the house were covered, including the *Prometheus* fire from heaven, self-taught piece —Copley's copy of the original— shrouded in white. When all were assembled and quiet, Dr. Besiegt stood. Regina, somberly dressed, with a white handkerchief balled in her hand, moved her knees just a bit to make room for him. I noticed that hand, not as coarse and red as my mother's but not soft and white, either. Victor's father had white fluffy hair worn in a tail like the father of our country, and was a bit stout, like his friend Dr. Kimball, who stood near the doorway of the front parlor.

Dr. Besiegt stood looking tenderly down on the younger of his sons for some moments. Then he turned just a bit but as though still speaking to his dear departed, and he said, "Father, have mercy on us who seem born but to nourish the ground. But how can it be? Those of us who loved Greenleaf come here to ask. We believe we have been made in thine image, and Greenleaf was made in thine image, and now we are consigning the remains of that dear image to the earth you have given us, to nourish it. Our Brother, the Lord Jesus, said that if we believe in him we would *never* die! Thus spoke your son in whom you were well pleased. Therefore, we believe his words against the experience of our senses which do indeed die as the body falls away. The life is more than raiment, and the body more than bread, for it is the house of our spirit. May Greenleaf be blessed in you forever, for now he is in *your* presence, with his mother Elizabeth, and gone out of this Gottheim where but part of his family yet dwells."

He looked up from the still face of Greenleaf, his gaze shifting a bit to one sitting by. He looked direct to Victor, whose dark eyes were glossy, his brow tormented. Victor did not look away. Softly Dr. Besiegt said, "We will believe it, amen."

Monster at the Ends of the Earth

Something moved off my left shoulder and I turned to catch sight of him running through the trees in morning light down toward the river; his yellow hair flying. I hollered and hefted the musket, following hard after. Behind me came the call echoing from man to man as they came running. I made it to the river to see him, small in the distance, dividing the waters beneath a wooded slope, trailing the wake of a powerful swimmer. I stopped to prepare the musket but the massive Loomis came up and had his ready and firing almost before I could prime the pan. Later, as I hurried on my last exhausting effort I would think that, indeed, I'd have sent my fire into him had I been as ready, no questions asked of myself. ...But then, again, I thought, *Or would I?* Still, I would be uncertain, even then.

Loomis, and one or two of the others, had missed their mark as it rounded the nearest bend. There were a series of bends on that stretch, with the feet of the mountains and knolls wading down into the Arossagunticook currents. Loomis had gone back a bit toward the house along the shore. From a low landing there, I watched him drive the canoe into the current, allowing but one other to go with him; the canoe he had earlier fetched from someone in the town. There was another, larger—from the household—and also a flat bottom rower. All these were loaded and gone off. I watched them work oars and paddles, soon to disappear around that first bend. I stood still a time, watching.

I was still standing there when Victor came up behind breathless and said, "They've gone wrong. He's already escaped them."

I swung round, a bit relieved to hear him say so for I had the strange calm feeling that I had done right not to follow... all the while wondering if I might not be an ass or a coward—these thoughts anchored in my complete vanity: What would they all think?

But my relief was short-lived, for then Victor said, "You need to watch by the house until they discover their error. We've got to go back."

Leaving the best help to their misbegotten chase, we tramped up toward the rutted road, it being easier here than threading back through the trees toward the house. Though it was morning the woods were high and darkling. We spoke almost not at all, Victor still trying to catch his breath. I was thinking, *He's right. The beast is too cunning. He let me see him, that's all.* I said, "We better run!" And off we went, still weaving among the trunks (Victor lagging a bit behind), and cutting off to make our separate ways around more thickets that had grown in amongst the blowdown.

Victor had almost caught up with me and as we came together around one giant white pine — next I know, he is there in our faces like the great mixed up mountain of mismatched anatomy he was— his wet hair a'swing with the force of his thrust in flinging me aside. I must have fallen with violence against the pine bole, for next I knew I was but slowly turning over in its crooks. From my knees I caught sight of his yellow hair flying, but what sickened me was recognition of the burden he bore. He disappeared among the woods but not before I saw his maker with struggling legs, swung from the cradle of the being's great arms to the back of his shoulder. Victor was on that monster's shoulder! — gripped in his powerful arm — taking a ride he had not looked for.

Still crawling about, I looked for the musket while trying to gain my legs and keep my eye on them. *How had he done it?* My only consolation, as at last I lay hands on the weapon, was that they fled away from the direction of the household. They were going into the wilderness beyond the road; and I was going after, still fumbling with the weapon and trying to get my gait. What help I had was the gap made in the trees where light now fell on the roadway. I saw him plain in the sunlight, crossing, moving into the woods again. Victor Besiegt looked like the slim bundle of a strawman, a scarecrow flopping, but pinned secure round his middle to the great and powerful fiend. The yellow hair flew in the light like a strange banner, a lurid banner from the nether regions, bright in those woodland shadows. If I continued now to regain strength and agility I might not be overburdened with difficulty in keeping up.

What, in the former thirteen colonies and the District of Maine, is he doing? I could not stop thinking of everything under the sun as the monster of Victor Besiegt carried him further up and into the wilderness of great Jasper Mountain. It was well into afternoon as we worked our way high beyond the village and were ascending in earnest. Would Loomis soon follow and help me? With all the care I took to keep the trail evident (meaning I took no care on the way), he should have no trouble tracking this odd trio: a thug monster, its maker, and me— the foolish work-shirking would-be poet. Then I recalled the up-current goose chase Loomis was on and wondered if it would help any for him to go into these woods after dark trying to find us.

And, I was certain, a storm was coming back on us from the great Gulf of Maine. It would soak us sure and send rivulets to wash out any trace I may have left in the mould. The wind had begun and as I climbed higher, hour on hour, most time keeping them in sight, I felt its keen edges.

The mind is a curious bucket of orts, entertaining all kinds of notions making their inroads helter-skelter, whether we would or no. The imagination can be a scary thing, or a wild or woolly recalcitrant romantic: welcoming of outlandish misconstructions. Grabbing hold on deadfall and great rocks, and working to keep the ungainly flintlock musket slung on my back, I thought, *If we had any inkling of how to control it or make it go this way or that, we would have such a job!* And, to my mind then, an unpleasant and onerous one. One thing that can help is the learning of poetry by rote, or what we called getting it by heart. That keeps the mind busy. But, then, if you don't watch, you recollect something like:

He took the children by the hand,
While teares stood in their eye,
And bade them come and go with him,
And look they did not crye:
And two long miles he ledd them on,
While they for food complaine:
"Stay here," quoth he, "I'll bring ye bread,
When I come back againe."
The prettye babes, with hand in hand,
Went wandering up and downe;
But never more they sawe the man
Approaching from the town.
Thus wandered these two prettye babes,
Till death did end their grief;
In one another's armes they dyed,
As babes wanting relief.
No burial these prettye babes
Of any man receives,
Till Robin-redbreast painfully
Did cover them with leaves.

Perhaps I needed something more cheerful. Just then an idiotic thought would slip in to entertain *me* (instead of vice versa), and I'd about howl and lose my footing: even as my pilgrim pioneer part kept at its strenuous task of keeping them in sight: The look of Victor bouncing willy-nilly on the monster's great shoulder, sometimes pinioned to its side, sometimes on its back or in its arms, would raise the howling laughter in my throat and I would just have to let fly. No doubt the brute kept track of my whereabouts in those moments. At least, till the wind began to rip away my laughter.

But yet there was an underlayer, at times a sick overlay also, of fearful dread; just pushing on me with deep concern for this man I had come to love. Victor. My brother. *I don't want to lose you like you have lost Greenleaf!* All my exertions on his behalf since that peculiar moment when I saw him beneath the pine with the white robin! I would come to understand that Abner would love his neighbor like his mother and sister when once he had exercised himself on his neighbor's behalf. Yet, just then in my struggles, it but knit me to him in some profound way that I did not think to fathom.

Do you wonder I could keep up, as up up we climbed? Me with the heavy and burdensome flintlock, monstrous rocks blocking the way? And the air was thinning out as higher and higher we strove. I had such *work* and the strength was sinking out of me, away. It began affecting my desire to help Victor, to do whatever it was I was trying *so* to do. This doing was fast becoming a thing of futility, hope and faith a spurious— Then I remembered my father on Benedict Arnold's revolutionary but disastrous trek through Maine to Québec, and the awful unknown country they had traversed just north and east of here, ill-starred quest of his army on the citadel perched high above the St. Lawrence. Oh that was a disaster of giant proportions. It weakened me to think of it. I will never forget mother telling me the men ate their shoes to stave off starvation. It all came into my beleaguered mind.

Then, along with it, came the part about the fir sap.

We had some way to go before climbing far above the trees on these mighty flanks— if that was his intention. We were yet in the tangles and steep places where one wonders how the great trees keep hold on the mountainside. Here was yet plentiful balsam fir where the weather and scant soil allowed. Above, such great trees as these would find no place at all and must suffer the insult of poor adaptation. A humility that the more adaptable but dwarfish crooked-wood endured by keeping low. But this was no land for the deceptively strong-looking mighty white pines! If there you tried to transplant such a giant, even in infancy, it would never live to be sublime. I cannot climb on Jasper Mountain without feeling its great antiquity and power. Enfeebling of even a young man in health such as I was that day.

I let them go on.

I stopped, gasping, looking up, seeing the bright flash of hair in the bright light and let them go. I sat down on what you might think an outcropping but was just an old great moss-grown stone left in the wake of the monstrous ice fields Dr. Kimball had told me of. I looked around, panting, and saw that balsam fir —and was going to devour it. Yes, that was a fancy born of my depletion. I stood, gained my legs, and went over to it, picking my way with hands and feet: lay my hand on its rough side and reached. Here were bark blisters ripe for the slitting. I slipped in my blade and let the sap down onto my tongue, carefully. I did this three or four times. This was the stuff to which father had attributed health to their party in its awful strait. I began to feel better but the light was now about gone.

Now, you may wonder at what happened next. No, I did not need another Indian. I might have. —If the wild victorious deep-throated crowing of Victor's monster had not come echoing down to me where I waited. That brute cry audibly showed me where he was above me. I half expected to hear the body of his maker come tumbling down through the great rocks and deadfall after the sound of that bellowing. The wind had carried it instead of obliterating, and I pricked up and stood staring.

Yes, you may wonder. I did not... not long enough, but maybe I should have. Even though there was no sense whatever in his machinations and motivations, that I could perceive.... It made perfect sense if I took into account the irrationality of a monster who thinks it can get something, or do anything worthwhile on a whim... with nought but brute strength. It would be all the same to me if he were setting up to make buckets of coin: What good would it do him in the long run? But, in fact, at that particular moment, as would be revealed, there was a *method* of madness in that cry.

I followed on until dark's descent with the clouds; and, as the snow fell, quiet ensued. Then his voice dropped down to me with the snowfall, thick and rich, its quality at first quiet and reasonable, almost soothing. But, where I sat listening among the rocks, its mismatch of syntax and tone put me on edge. Why was he now speaking so? Except for his childlike constructions, his intonation was almost like a learned man in a robe with wig, or a professor, lecturer of some kind.

I sat among little firs here in the rocks. They comforted and helped hold my warmth to me. There fell a quiet snow, as is not uncommon in our late New England springs, especially here in the northern District of Maine on a mountain. But I sat up straight to hear as he began telling the story of Adam and Eve, our founding folk and origination story here in the West. I had forgotten that this story first came of the Hebrews in the Holy Land of the East; where heat, desert, salt flats, salt seas and strange valleys cleave the earth.

"Yes, Abner," came his deep full reasonable voice down to me with the thick snow. "I know the stories. I learned from Bible, your holy scriptures. Father Griswold would read us every Sunday as I sat quiet, listening on the stair below, in the cellar. You were told by God that you would die and you died. Everyone of you dies.... Maker says I am dead. I'm no good I'm of dead people, ones you had to throw away."

Good gracious, I thought, He's taken on his maker's mental posture of reasonableness... all of a sudden. I called up to him, "Our ancestors were tempted to believe they wouldn't die of the knowledge of good and evil. Now their descendents are told they will not live afterward. Both are the lies of the devil, Mr. Monster!"

There! I had done it. It was the first time I had said anything to him. Now I was talking like Abner talks to Victor —and what in the United States of America was I doing that for!? *He is a monster* an unreasonable monster and up to no good! We are on Jasper Mountain, not sitting in the schoolhouse. This mountain can kill us without so much as thinking about it.

The snow was falling in quiet bucketfuls. Upon the summit was a snowcap left over from winter. In some reaches and niches there might be snow from two years ago. I hunkered beneath the skimpy boughs as best I could and was grateful for my big-brimmed buckskin hat. Nevertheless I was sodden and soaking up the damp.

The monster was laughing—that terrifying bellow alternating with shrieks which had never accorded with his rich voice.

"Abner Bartlett the schoolboy! My maker's pupil who belongs on a farm!"

"We grow all the food you can eat, Mr. Monster! There's very little food for folks who don't grow their own!" *Without us*, I thought but did not add.

Then he began on a regular litany of my defects. I was hard put to know how it came by so much knowledge of me. All the silly little stories of my foolish existence. Like the time I wasted shot on a skunk for no reason, the smell of which tainted Beatrice's milk. Or when I wrote a ballad on the teacher and Henry Howe took and put it on his desk. How about the time I wasted an afternoon chopping ants down the middle? Cruelties and stupidities... maybe from the time I was first introduced to the privy, until now.

Suddenly Victor's voice came down, hoarse and broken, without force. But I did make out the words *pay no mind*, and *gossip*. The awful bellow followed and I shivered where I crouched.

Next the monster began mocking everyone in the village, by name. Seemed he knew all about Ham Bean, Dr. Kimball and his kinsman, and the others. He called them all piss-poor. Then he did the same with the names of Greenleaf and Regina. Knocked all these worthy people up one side and down the other. (Which the townsfolk themselves had already done for one another, I guess.)

"Victor Besiegt is the piss of the piss-poor!" This he exclaimed with most relish. "He makes a monster and wants to wash the monster away from his hands!"

I sat down here among the rocks and puckerbrush and heard all the good things people did turned on their heads with evil motives imputed: Regina fed the poor so she would look good to the neighbors, and to make believe she'd get a crown in heaven when she died. Dr. Besiegt made work for men because he could get rich off their labor and send his son to college. Greenleaf was an idol worshiper, such as God condemned and would thank the monster for putting him in hell. Then he started on my mother and Philippa, saying the first was a coot and a battle-axe who destroyed me with her drudgery. Philippa, he said, had too many children. "God said multiply and she made more people to go in the ground."

Then I stood up and shouted something unfit and began climbing toward them through the pouring snow. The musket hung heavy and I realized I could never use it in such a rage and storm... but here is *the hatchet!* I felt the cold iron in my belt, making sure of it.

But the monster, carrying his prize, climbed on ahead of me. After a scramble among the wet rocks, I sank down and let the emotional fever die in the cold and dark.

After a bit the voice came down through the falling snow. "God made Victor Besiegt, a man who believes not in him. What piss is a man, God made. Man is full of stupidity, does things but no things last he does. When little he is helpless and stupid. Monster will stomp their stupid small heads."

"Don't listen, Abner!" Victor's voice sounded. I thought of the times Victor had stymied me with his arguments —words—and felt he knew my weaknesses and was now trying to arm me against such from his monster.

"Monster is better than what God made. Monster can do all he wants. I am already dead. Man can do nothing but grow old and die. He can pretend he will do good and live long but man is always sick, feeble, dies—What image is that? What's this dead feeble God? What? My maker belongs to me. I can do what I want with him. There is no good no evil only monster. Monster is the good and evil. Foolish Abner. All is monster's. I make my own brides."

"Don't drop your guard!"

With that a great sound of cracking and breaking of limbs and rocks came down to me through the snowfall. I thought sure then Victor was being destroyed. Everything grew quiet and I heard no more for awhile. I fingered the hatchet. I was so weary. Was this mountain going to help or hinder me? Was Victor hurt, dead?

"Victor! Victor!"

Then I heard it, not but a croak. "...Abner...."

At length I heard the subdued voice of his monster. "Go to sleep Abner. We will talk in the morning."

Go to sleep Abner we will talk in the morning?

Oh Lord, I prayed. *What* is this monster?

But I did go to sleep, all huddled together. And the snow fell down.

I heard a noise. Not knowing what it was, I sat up, thinking, He's come down to see if I'm awake. Pale early light shone through the snow of my covering here in a patch of small spruce. Quietly I slipped the buckskin covering from the barrel and pointed the muzzle out through the branches and snow, then I showed the barrel a bit more in the direction it seemed he was coming. Now I was sure of his movements, and that he had stopped. Now he was going back up in almost the same way he had come down. I sat back relieved, no further lesson in waking up needed. So much for his little morning talk. I smiled grimly.

For the first time since leaving my post at the funeral, I took my opportunity to check the musket's readiness for firing. I saw that whoever had cleaned it up last had laid in a bead of grease between barrel and forearm in front of the lock. Good. This would help with the firing in the wet weather but I would be keeping the muzzle down till then all the same. There was also a bit of grease about the pan. The main charge was already in, and the barrel clean as a whistle so the charge would be dry. With the pan in such shape and the priming powder dry in its pouch on the string round my neck, I was now set.

I was still worried about Victor. Then I heard him calling to me. I climbed out into a world of whiteness and purity. I began climbing, following them through the snow and fallen woodland wreckage, climbing and climbing in the pure air until at last the tangle of big trees was below and all that remained was the snow-covered world of the mountain's head above us. The air was thin. I was breathing as though with a hand pressed on my chest. The summit was still a long way off and I did not think the monster would climb up there—what reason would he have for it? He could kill Victor at any moment, and if he aimed well with my poor friend's body, he could 'most kill me at the same time. I felt in the monster's erratic desperation a murderous rage, sometimes laced with cunning, and had no expectations except that whatever was in store would be startling in high degree.

On and on we climbed. Once I turned back briefly to catch a breath and saw the whole blue world spread out below. There were the threads of the river gleaming here and there, and the great forests and hills, smoky haze curling out where I knew there would be Gottheim edging the valley of the ponds. I turned back and scrambled as best I could over the slippery rocks and snow.

Suddenly, I came upon Victor lying in the snow behind a boulder. My glance shot ahead toward the monster above, his yellow hair streaming out on the wind of the mountain. I knelt down beside Victor but he struggled up, cut and bruised. He was gasping for breath, more from urgency, I suspected than from his ordeal.

"It's not me he wants, Abner! It's you! You are the one he's going to kill. It's all a ploy to kill you!"

In a flash about like what you get in the pan, I saw it was so, and that this was the method of his madness coming to fruition. I made a promise without thinking: "I'm going to get him first."

"He could get you no other way than to lure you to the ends of the earth – this mountain. ...He knows you love me and is jealous beyond bearing. ...He will crush you the moment he has the chance.... Me he will keep for his sick fancy — *it's you*, with your tenacious goodness, he wants to kill.... Abner, he is the natural man fully ripe! ...He was crying because I could not be a father to him!... He just has no idea *how to be*."

He lay back, dazed, his strength spent.

I looked up then to see the back of the monster still climbing up through the snow. Should I follow or stay here with Victor? I decided I could not stay, much as I wanted to take Victor down to safety. The sooner I got this over with the sooner I could take him back home and perhaps avoid a deadly chill and fever. The difficulty of conscience I had experienced at the point of killing before did not even enter my head at that time. Simply, I began again crawling my way up the backside of great Jasper Mountain, through the cold and the rocks, over the crunchy crooked woods, laden with snow. But suddenly there he was ahead, standing above in the snow as though waiting for me.

With no time to prime or take my stance I looked up to see him charge. His yellow hair flew out like a cape behind as he charged down toward me screaming like a mechanical thing, his disjoins flailing and arms thrashing. My heart and nerve melted at the sight. Yet out the corner of my eye I saw something. Attracted by the monster's flailing, it came into full view, a raccoon, its moving paws a blur— churning through snow over the small crooked treetops.

What's it doing up here? Came the idiotic thought into my head.

Raccoons are big things, bigger than you'd expect from their pictures, and never easily intimidated. Even so, on seeing such a monster, it should have run off. Not this one. Following the rule of the disease, it went like a machine itself straight for him and took hold of his leg in its jaws. The monster fell and began rolling, trying to loose this giant-sized burr, breaking up the crooked-wood in his mighty throes.

I had no time to be puzzled: those massive hands and thews would have it loose: I put down my head, primed the pan, poised the barrel and aimed. The turmoil and cacophony of their struggle did not distract me. I whispered. "*Father forgive him! He knows not what he's done!*" I dropped the hammer on the cock, giving fire in one shattering explosion. Through an acrid cloud of smoke and vapor I saw blood pouring through the monster's yellow hair at the back of his neck, soaking, but the raccoon held on. The great one's thrashing ceased, and I heard the critter snarling and gurgling, still clenched on Victor's monster. I jerked the blade of the borrowed hatchet from my belt, and flung it with all my might into the raccoon's head. Dead on at seventy paces. I had done them both nearly in the same bodily spot and was so joyful I leapt in the air.

"Oh, Father! You should've seen it!" My father had been on Arnold's expedition but, more importantly, he had fought at the rail fence. The Battle of Bunker Hill had the status of awful patriotic mythology, the *true thing*, and I knew he would be glad of me. You know, of course, now, that my father did see me, but I had no inkling at that moment.

Next thing I had left the musket and was climbing up the slippery rocks to them. The snow began falling again. Was I thinking, now in some leisure, *Glory, glory, I got the monster, I got the monster, you helped me finally get the monster?* No, I was thinking, *Watch now. Clean that blade before all else, it's hydrophobic.*

That is how we Gott'imites do in the wilderness: Forget Glory. Let us just survive.

Aftermath

I stood looking down at him.

Here surely should have been the material for it, I had the mind and sensibility for it, but I never became that great poet, having no real faculty for that highest of literary forms. I would see much in my life after that. I would be educated in the little college down east, Bowdoin, where many famous men of profound skill, learning, gifts and understanding would begin their long careers: Longfellow, Hawthorne, President Pierce, the great Joshua Chamberlain who successfully led the defense of Little Round Top during the Battle of Gettysburg; the Arctic explorer Admiral Robert Perry and many others, all to attend, long after I graduated, in its ascendancy to an Ivy League school. Because of the work my father did as an ordinary soldier in the Revolution, the two men I most admired in the town, Drs. Besiegt and Kimball, would see to the scholarship. I would be among those with Professor Abbott to make the surveying trek of the school's West and East Grants in the wilds of the interior, laying first European-descended eyes, with them, on Gulf Hagas (a wonderment of nature). Not far from that great gorge would build itself in the wilderness the great blast furnace and coke ovens of the Katahdin Ironworks, smelting pig iron and drawing workmen into the wild from the corners of New England. And I would see the advance of the great Industrial Revolution with its many attendant haphazard miracles and haphazard debasements: All this: But I have never seen anything like that monster.

In death he was as appalling as in life, an immense museum piece specimen, too great to be stuffed and displayed in the case in Dr. Kimball's beautiful Federal-style house. Later I would come to think that I would have liked to measure his dimensions, but at that moment of deep, bone deep, relief, I could not think of it. I could think of nothing. The fearless and diseased raccoon beast, now dead, still glommed onto his leg. The monster, of distorted proportions, lay sprawled and misshapen in the dark-stained snow; like so much woodland wreckage felled by this mighty mountain: Thought was taken away for that moment, leaving only wonder in its wake.

I stooped and hacked off a small token of his anatomy. Then I went back down over the slippery rocks looking for Victor. I found him looking dazed. One eye was starting to blacken and swell and there was a cut above it. He was leaning against a rock, his knees up, legs apart. His hands lay calmly clasped between them. He whispered, "I heard the shot." Thinking to set his mind to rest, and give peace at last, I showed him the token.

He was slow to recognize or seize on its significance. He drew back. "What... what is it?" But he knew.

"His ring finger," I answered.

He looked away. He was silent again, then lay his head back on the rock, closing haggard, troubled eyes. After a bit he said, "Thank you, Abner."

My heart was full of tenderness and love for him. I said, "Don't you see, Victor? Now that he is dead....With this finger for token no one need ever know. They'll think I killed the extortionist 'thug,' and left him up here because it was too much trouble to bring him down. They will not know. That you made him. ...Look, friend. You are going to live now. You are going to marry Regina. You will have a family!" I had expected a deep sense of relief, maybe even great happiness coming to him in these words. But he said,

"No, Abner." He looked up at me. "You are not going to besmirch your integrity for this. You have kept to it through all kinds of hazard, and great exertion. Let it continue on. And on." Again he closed his eyes and lay back.

Then he said, "The finger is good.... What we will do.... You must give me something, strengthen me, and we will go up to him. You still have your journal?"

"It was given me of mother when she helped get me out of Dr. Kimball's cellar.... I've wondered since then if she may have looked into it. If she knows anything of this." I gestured toward the white summit with my hand. Did she know how I really had to wrestle with it all, not just the false accusation? But then I recalled her dry remark about Victor's legs and thought, No. Her concern was always a burden, but now I had a new appreciation of her trust.

"...I will sketch him, as a specimen.... With my pencil I have somewhere." He began to feel for the pockets in his mourning clothes. "And you will make notes. —I am quite good at getting the likeness of a specimen, as long as it is dead, still before me to study. I cannot draw living animated things. Dr. Kimball, I think, will believe us." He was still a bit dazed. "The hardest thing.... –My father. Think of the difference between me and Dr. Besiegt as fatherly types. You attributed to me the desire to help others live long, maybe even help them achieve immortality. But Abner, I have a distinct memory of glorying so in my work, being so ready to receive glory for it." His gaze had been withdrawn, but now he looked up at me.

"I have stupid thoughts, too, Victor. They are but the tares that grow up with the wheat."

He was silent, then he smiled a bit. "...How were you able to—? Did he—?"

I told him then about the rabid raccoon led by its disease, and my diagnosis of it. He readily agreed with me and warned about the blade. I was able to reassure him on that account. He seemed desirous to make sure of it.

We made our halting way back down through the snow, having collected the proofs needed for Lewis Loomis. If that one were interested, he could climb up here himself to prove with his own eyes the outrageous creation of Victor Besiegt. I kept wondering how it would all work out but remained silent out of respect for my friend's grief and bemusement. Thinking of Greenleaf and his own guilt: It cannot have been easy for him to face the conversations he must have with Regina and his father. I was still burdened with the borrowed weapons, and we had to make our way through deep snow, an afternoon and overnight. Before we were well out of it, I had to make a fire to warm Victor, who was yet wearing his good clothes, garments in which he had buried his brother. For the first time I made him laugh by telling him about my adventures trying to get the crazy white little old man corralled, fed, made warm and safe; and how he had instead lead me home.

We did meet the lawman, along with some others, coming up through the woodland, a good piece above where the village can be bypassed on the way to Besiegt's. Loomis seemed to show a new respect for me, perhaps because I had shown understanding of the thug's cunning. Victor was ailing, so I gave Loomis the token, told him the monster was dead, and proposed to take Victor home. He did not bat an eye over the word monster, most likely assuming I meant the thug. Then he and one other turned and followed up the way they had seen us come down. The others went back toward Gott'im, talking, talking. I wished Loomis well in my heart, but had not much hope he would find the body up there. It's a big mountain.

You will be wondering about the reconciliation of Victor and his father, maybe? I was not privy to that. But I will tell you that after we got back and had a meal of Regina's preparing, from the leftover funeral feast, I saw the two men walking together in the distance, going down through the trees toward the river. One was an old man, with fluffy white hair like a halo round his head. He was good and wise, full of able guidance. And no doubt forgiving. The other had more than enough to learn of him. Victor would need that forgiveness. There was much to forgive.

Yes, Regina and Victor married. He continued his studies but did not apply them. He wrote, but not about *that*, although he encouraged me to: "He was my Demogorgon, Abner. Brought to life from the pre-logical regions. If you were ever to comprehend the thing in imaginative verse it would help others grasp the significance of what we are about with our scientific applications. Who will be wise enough to guide us?"

He wrote that the story of Genesis was a mythological compression of an immense extrapolation by God using God's expressed laws of nature, some of which seem to us irrational. I believe this is what he turned his mind to in all his later inquiries... encouraged by the many studies in biology of great thinkers of the age. And Victor did eventually answer my question concerning his use of various people to fashion his monster instead of trying to revive a single corpse. You remember he was a monster of many parts. But aside from the question of death by disease, as opposed to injury (which meant using carefully selected specimens), Victor was fearful of bringing to life an extant soul. He had reasoned that a whole corpse would have a mind desiring to continue with its own familial life. In this he acknowledged the mystery of the human soul.

I stood watching father and son disappear together through the trees. Then I turned and went along the lane through the budding lilac bushes off toward the road. My mother was waiting; and all that needs doing on a farm in spring.

~~~~~~~~~~~~~~~~~

The God's Cycle is set in the early mid-1980s
    Five books in THE GOD'S CYCLE
    God's House:
    Return to God's House
    Within Without
    In Winter

God's Wilderness:
    Mystery Gottheim
    Balder's Wilderness
    Plus
    Gott'im's Monster

THE GOD'S CYCLE is composed in two themes, *God's House* and *God's Wilderness*, each divided into three books. Its fantastic elements sparse in beginning, the cycle moves through its story in time and place with increasing mythic emphasis. Then time and place are no more, and its hero, Balder Simon, must transit the dim and curious mists of pure story.

Also by S. Dorman: *FANTASTIC TRAVELOGUE: Mark Twain and CS Lewis Talk Things Over in The Hereafter.*
~~~~~~~~~~~~~~~~~

From The God's Cycle
Balder's Wilderness

He turned over and sat still in the sodden leaves, leaning against the fallen tree. Blinking, rubbing his cheek. Daniel....

Dazed, now he felt more than saw the light behind him. Or maybe he saw its beam falling on his legs, or down below him across the wooded slope. He turned. The star was up there again. But he didn't think long about it because a man was stepping long-legged down toward him, a shadow, a shape. Not Charlie, he knew. Not the right size or shape, that silhouette. Not that of a small man in the black pajamas of the VC, but tall. Now he saw the felt hat and buckskin of a... what? Back-to-the-lander? One of that homesteader woman's friends up from Chesterville way? He carried a long vintage rifle of some sort and spoke out kinda friendly. Normally Balder would have asked about that rifle right off. Maybe, what kind of spin-drift did projectile forces give its ball?

"You the man looking for his lost son?" He said out, no longer just a silhouette and, yes, wearing real buckskin. Needed a shave. Having come down from above, the man stood now below him in the lit drizzle.

He did not offer him a hand. Balder jumped up, nearly losing his footing in his earnestness to stand. He could almost have reached out to touch him; to touch or maybe test his reality. The man slid his rifle to his back, hanging on a leather strap. Maybe it should've been sheathed. Balder wondered vaguely if he had been hunting. That was no bird gun though. It was bird season.

Balder nearly shouted. "They find him?!"

The man had circled swiftly back round him and now stood just above again and backlit, the soft fine slow rain like a nimbus around him, dirty drizzle jumping off him as though he were crystal and not a sopping piece of flesh.

"No!... Well, I mean...."

His voice fell.

" —What?" Balder said it with urgency. "He's—" Balder stopped. "No-no," the man was quick to say. "That is, I did not find his body... if that

worries you."

"His name is Daniel, you heard? Will you keep looking? He's been out too long in this— 'less they found him." His voice dropped. "They might'a." There was no note of hope. Balder's was the most unbelieving voice you could fear to hear. The man's breath fell on Balder in a cloud.

Balder looked up toward the light. "Not finding a body.... That's a good thing." He looked down from there on the shade of the man outlined in dancing wet light. "Is that a searchlight, you think?—You know?"

The man said nothing. Just stood there in a stance to hold onto the hillside, arms akimbo, rifle at his back, regarding him. He seemed almost as though listening for something, poised. Balder gathered the swift impression despite his thoughts for Daniel. He could not really see the man. He was almost all shadow.

Balder, at once defeated and determined, stepped around him and mounted, trudging, toward the light. It gleamed out very bright but peculiarly. Not glaring. Not as though shouting, exposing all in its swath. It had the calm white purity of a star but, as said, its light was falling as from the moon over all in its way. Yet it was not moon-cold but soft and wholesome. It made Balder feel better seeing it there.

Daniel, he said to himself. Then the light moved softly away. It seemed to slip off backward, as he moved, through the tree limbs and trunks, to slip down behind the shoulder of the mountainside. It was gone. The drizzle fell coldly, unlit, adding more to the twilight.

He stood contemplating. It was hardly spoken, the thought merely escaping like breath through his lips: "Oh, Daniel." Quietly. Wondering, and not entirely grievous.